Jeannie Renamo's List of Contenders:

WEALTHY BACHELOR #1:

Duncan Fox, Hot-Blooded Blue Blood
Attribute: Devastatingly handsome face
Fault: Alarmingly touchy-feely hands

WEALTHY BACHELOR #2:

Elliot Daniels, Newly Eligible Financier
Attribute: Sweet disposition
Fault: Still sweet on his ex

WEALTHY BACHELOR #3:

Stuart Singleton, Globe-Trotting Philanthropist
Attribute: Mr. Nice Guy
Fault: Mr. No Sparks

WEALTHY BACHELOR #4:

Kyle Hunter, Maddeningly Smug
Millionaire—and Boss
Attribute: He's got it all…looks, charm
and sex appeal
Fault: There must be *something*
that disqualifies him as
marriage material…or could
he be "the one" after all?

Dear Reader,

Romance in the workplace. Everyone says it shouldn't happen—and everyone knows it happens anyway. I currently work in an office full of women—no hope of romance there. But I remember one summer when I was cashiering at the local grocery store to earn extra money for college—and to pay for my horse. The manager was one of those good-looking flirts with a smile to die for. Unfortunately, he flirted with everyone and went further with no one. But I do remember how flattered I was when my parents came up to school to visit me and he'd sent along a bouquet. (Of daisies, mind you, but flowers all the same.) Anyway, Jeannie Renamo, heroine of Lynda Simons' *Marrying Well*, has a lot better luck with her boss. Kyle Hunter is, quite simply, the perfect man for her—something they're both about to find out.

And then there's Toni Collins' newest, *The Almost-Perfect Proposal.* It takes a fifty-year-old proposal gone astray to introduce Amy Barrington to Brian Reynolds, but it's clearly not going to take Brian another fifty years to utter a proposal of his own. Sometimes it's a good thing the mail isn't always reliable!

Enjoy both these wonderful books, and rejoin us next month here at Yours Truly, because we'll be bringing you two more books about unexpectedly meeting, dating— and marrying!—Mr. Right.

Leslie Wainger,
Senior Editor and Editorial Coordinator

Please address questions and book requests to:
Silhouette Reader Service
U.S.: 3010 Walden Ave., P.O. Box 1325, Buffalo, NY 14269
Canadian: P.O. Box 609, Fort Erie, Ont. L2A 5X3

LYNDA SIMONS

Marrying Well

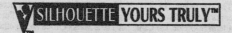

Published by Silhouette Books
America's Publisher of Contemporary Romance

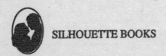 SILHOUETTE BOOKS

ISBN 0-373-52042-5

MARRYING WELL

About the author

"No, I did not marry a rich man. Not that I planned it that way. If truth be told, he promised on bended knee that he would be rich one day. Rockefeller rich, if I remember correctly. And, child bride that I was, I believed him.

"Twenty years later, I still believe him. And so do our two daughters. But no one is holding their breath. In fact, we all exhaled a long time ago, because life is just too short to waste waiting for anything.

"So instead we canoe in the summer, hike in the winter and when we're all too lazy for either, we sit in the dark in our lovely two-story mortgage and watch movies. In those rare moments when I'm not closeted away with my computer obsessing over a story, we argue about whose turn it is to do dishes and whether or not washing machines really eat socks. And if my husband never becomes a rich man? At least we all know I married well."

For Dot and Bill, with love

1

Marrying Well
(A Practical Guide)

by

Lady Victoria Boulderbottom

Step One: Overcoming Guilt

This month's column is dedicated to those of you who have had it up to here with low-budget dreamers. It's for those women who are ready to seriously undertake the task of finding a rich husband, but aren't sure how to go about it.

I know some of you may secretly long to pursue this noble tradition, but have a problem with guilt. This is understandable.

We do, after all, live in a society that loves to point a nasty finger and holler, "She only married him for the money," anytime some nice girl hits it big.

So guilt will be the first issue we'll deal with today. Once you've conquered that, there will be no stopping you.

Now I want you all to stand proudly in front of a mirror, take a deep breath and repeat these words:

Love, schmuv. He's rich and I want him.

Kyle popped out the disk and tossed it across his desk. "I can't run this. The whole idea is ludicrous."

Outside, the wind shifted, driving the warm spring rain against the glass. Jeannie stepped away from the window, turning her back on one storm to face another.

"Have I mentioned how good it is to have you back, Kyle?" She sank into the chair opposite him and smiled. "How long are you staying?"

He glanced up. "As long as it takes."

"Wonderful," Jeannie muttered as the phone started to ring.

Kyle picked up the receiver. "Hold on a minute, please." Cupping a hand over the mouthpiece, he nodded at the disk. "Take that with you when you go," he said to Jeannie, then swung the chair around so his back was to her. He lowered his voice. "Hunter here, how can I help you?"

Jeannie rose and snapped up the disk, tapping it against her palm as she paced back and forth in front of the desk. *Take that with you when you go.* No discussion, no compromise, nothing. The man hadn't changed a bit.

She'd been expecting this, of course. In the days following his return to Chicago, Kyle had managed to alienate the art director, the advertising manager and most of the department heads as he undertook a complete revamping of his magazine.

As editor of *Aspects'* Single Life section, how could she hope to fare any differently?

She paused and looked over at him.

Tall, blond and blue eyed, the legendary Kyle Hunter was still undeniably good-looking. His skin was tanned, his shoulders broader than she remembered and the power suits had been abandoned in favor of a pair of khakis and a loose cotton shirt.

Whatever he'd been doing in Maine for the past two years had definitely agreed with him, Jeannie decided. And the sooner he went back to it, the better.

Kyle ended the call and turned back to his computer. "The issue is closed," he said, not bothering to look up as Jeannie approached.

She set the disk in front of him and sat down. "You know, Kyle, for a man of vision you can be remarkably shortsighted."

He lifted his head. "Is that so?"

Jeannie remembered that gaze—intense and unwavering, daring her to turn away. So she propped her elbows on the desk and met it squarely. "What else do you call it when someone rejects an article he hasn't even read?"

He swiveled the chair around to face her. "What makes you think I haven't read it?"

"You haven't had time. You weren't in here more than five minutes when I came in."

One brow raised. "I had no idea I was being kept under such close scrutiny."

Jeannie laughed easily. "Don't flatter yourself. I just happened to be coming back from lunch with Magda when you went by." She reached out and gave the disk a spin. "How much did you read?"

"Enough to know it won't work."

"Why not?"

"Because it's not your usual Boulderbottom stuff." The faintest trace of a smile curved his lips as he leaned closer. "What were you thinking about anyway?"

His tone was so low, it bordered on intimate, and Jeannie found herself bending to him, her response as instinctive as it was unsettling. She eased back in the seat, reminding herself that Kyle was a man best dealt with firmly but from a distance.

"A Boulderbottom spoof. You know, a parody, biting satire...that sort of thing." She nudged the disk toward him. "Keep reading. You'll catch on."

His gaze drifted down to the small black square that sat between them. "Don't count on it."

"I have faith. Just read."

He flashed her one of his rare, charming smiles. "Forget it, Jeannie."

She crossed her legs and folded her hands in her lap. "I'm not leaving till you do."

The smile broadened. "Suit yourself."

Jeannie bristled. Kyle had the deepest dimples of any man she'd ever met. And the longer he sat there grinning at her, the more she remembered how much she truly disliked dimples on a man.

He stroked a hand across his chin. Eyes that reminded him of melting caramel watched his every move, their challenge clear and direct. He'd been expecting this, of course.

His last publisher, Marcus Underwood, had graciously attached performance reviews to each personnel file before running off with a sleeping bag and a rifle to take on the Alaskan outback.

It was the worst case of mid-life crisis Kyle had ever seen. But the reviews had evidently been written during one of Marcus's more lucid moments and were proving to be invaluable in helping him make decisions. The only one that was no use at all was Jeannie Renamo's.

Kyle had expected pages regarding her inability to grasp the concept of "no." Instead, "Watch her" was all Marcus had written. What was that supposed to mean? Kyle wondered. Watch out for her? Watch over her? As she shifted in the seat across from him, making her skirt ride up even higher on her thighs, it occurred to him that maybe it simply meant "Look at her"—something that was far too easy to do.

She'd only been with *Aspects* six months when he left, yet he'd remembered her the moment she walked into the first editorial meeting after his return. The same fiery curls, a face that was more arresting than beautiful and a style that could only be called eclectic. Lace and pin-stripes one day, wildflowers and a straw hat the next. How fitting that she'd chosen leather and steel that morning.

Jeannie crossed her legs, tapped her fingers on the arm-rest and tugged the zipper on her jacket down a little lower. Kyle leaned the chair way back and laced his fingers behind his head. This would be torture for her, just sitting and waiting—something else that hadn't changed.

Full of restless enthusiasm, she was always in motion—pacing while she talked on the phone, fidgeting with a pen during meetings. She put him in mind of a butterfly, all flash and movement. Fascinating to watch but impossible to follow, never lighting anywhere long enough to be caught.

Not that he wanted to. A woman like Jeannie would be too much work. Granted, there had been times when he had wondered what it would be like to hold her still and have her concentrate that energy on him.

But right now, all Kyle had time to think about was the magazine. And how quickly he could get away again.

Under Marcus's direction, *Aspects* had grown and prospered, but somewhere along the way the magazine had lost its edge. Once a bold and controversial publication, *Aspects* was now mired firmly in the middle of the road.

Kyle intended to put some fire back into the magazine before turning it over to someone else again. And the fact that he had to be in Maine by Labor Day meant the changes would have to be accomplished quickly. If that meant offending some of the staff as well as a few readers in the process, so be it. And Miss Renamo was no exception.

As if reading his thoughts, she dropped her head back and sighed heavily. "God, how I miss Marcus."

Kyle let the chair up slowly. "I'll bet. I understand Marcus was a real pushover in the last year."

Jeannie's eyes narrowed as she raised her head. "Marcus Underwood was a reasonable man. You, on the other hand, are impossible."

"Look, Jeannie," Kyle said patiently, knowing it would only irritate her further. "I know you've always thought of Victoria as your personal territory—"

She cut him off with a wave of her hand. "Hold it right there. Victoria *is* my territory. I created her, remember? And as I recall it, you fought me on that idea, as well. But perhaps you've managed to forget."

Kyle laughed softly. "How could I? It's been a while, but let's see if I can get this right." He started to quote.

> "'Lady Victoria Boulderbottom, a transmigrating turn-of-the-century spirit, finds herself caught in a time warp and winds up stranded inside a Chicago singles bar on a Saturday night. Never one to miss an opportunity, Victoria sheds her inhibitions along along with her corsets, and sets out to explore her newfound freedom.'"

He sat back. "How was that?"

"Not bad," Jeannie admitted, smiling in spite of herself.

She'd only been with the magazine three weeks when she'd approached him with the idea. Kyle's response had been typical. "Sorry, Jeannie. The idea just isn't right for *Aspects*."

"Of course it is," she'd insisted. "Victoria will bring a whole new perspective to the 'Single Life' section. Everything will be new to her. She'll be like a kid in a candy store. She won't know what to try first."

As usual, Kyle had been adamant. So Jeannie had pulled out her wallet and slapped five ten-dollar bills down on the desk.

"Here's the deal," she'd told him. "Fifty bucks says Victoria will be a hit first time out, and she'll still be holding her own six months later."

At a loss for only a moment, Kyle had recovered beautifully, stuffing the bills into his pocket and muttering, "You're on."

Just as Jeannie had predicted, *Aspects'* readers had taken immediately to Victoria's unique blend of naive innocence and wanton lust.

Within weeks, Lady Victoria Boulderbottom had become one of *Aspects'* most widely read columns, leaving Kyle red faced and Jeannie fifty dollars richer.

And if she wasn't mistaken, he had just trapped himself again.

She traced a line on the disk with a fingertip, her eyes following the movement. "In other words, you admit your first reaction to Victoria was wrong."

"I admitted that a long time ago."

"So there's a good chance you're wrong now too." She looked up at him. "Wouldn't you agree?"

His mouth quirked up on one side. "Nice try, Jeannie, but it won't work. 'Marrying Well' is pure fantasy. Women marry for money all the time—everyone knows that. But there's no tradition, no steps to follow that will guarantee success."

She shook her head in disbelief. "It's a spoof. Remember? It's not supposed to guarantee success."

"That's another problem. Everything else you've done

with her, even the most outlandish things, have been practical. Doable, if you know what I mean."

"Doable?"

"Like the time she took out all those personal ads in the newspapers and then wrote about the men she met. Great stuff, funny as hell, but practical."

"And you had doubts about that one, too, as I remember."

He gazed at the ceiling for a moment then drew in a deep breath and started again. "The point is that anyone could have read the article then gone out and placed their own ads knowing some of the pitfalls in advance, because Victoria had paved the way. That's what she does. It's the reason she's so popular." He smiled. "Don't fight it, Jeannie. Work with it."

Only through a conscious effort did Jeannie keep her seat.

In the last three months alone, she had worn love amulets, joined dating clubs and endured more cups of coffee with unmemorable men than she cared to remember. All in the name of research for Lady Victoria Boulderbottom. But more importantly, Jeannie read the letters that were sent to Victoria.

Women responded to her in a way Jeannie had never dreamed possible. Some told her their most intimate and heartbreaking stories while others simply wrote to express outrage with something she had done.

For the most part, however, the letters were from women who were simply happy to know they weren't the only ones meeting more than their share of less-than-wonderful men. Victoria's appeal lay in the fact that she was one of them—just another woman in the hope of finding true love, poking her curious nose into all the spots where men were rumored to be hiding. And having the grace to laugh when things went wrong.

If anyone understood what made the Boulderbottom

column successful, it was Jeannie. And the last thing she needed was advice from Kyle.

"I do work with her," she told him. "Every day. And I know 'Marrying Well' is perfect for Victoria."

Kyle rubbed a hand over his face. "What makes you so sure?"

"Instinct and experience."

Kyle shook his head. "Not good enough, Jeannie. Not anymore." Reaching across the desk, he selected a disk from a box and set it in front of her. "I want you to take a look at this."

She eyed the square uneasily. "What is it?"

"A new series for you and Victoria." Kyle turned back to the keyboard, letting her know there was no room for further argument. "The outline is quite extensive, but if you have any questions, we can go over them later."

Her hands tightened into fists on the arms of her chair. "I have a question now," she said evenly. "Why didn't you discuss the idea with me first?"

"I didn't feel there was any need."

"No need? This is my column we're talking about. A column that has done extremely well without any input from you in over two years."

Kyle faced her. "Don't push too far, Jeannie."

"I think I'm finally beginning to understand. It wouldn't have mattered what I put on your desk, would it? You would have rejected it anyway."

"You're wrong," Kyle said mildly. "If I felt the article had merit, I would print it and simply postpone the new series."

"But you still wouldn't have discussed it with me."

"No."

"Why not?"

"Because to be perfectly blunt, I don't have time. You were at the editorial meeting. You know the changes I want to see at *Aspects,* and right now, that's the only thing on my mind. My concern is what's good for the magazine. Nothing more."

She rose slowly, put one fingertip on his disk and slid it back. "And mine is what's good for Victoria."

Kyle's expression remained dangerously neutral. "Take a moment to think about it, Jeannie."

Now what? she wondered, as she crossed to the credenza. Kyle had always had a talent for reading a market—there was no denying that. Maybe his idea for a series had merit. But she resented the fact that it was a done deal.

Marcus had always discussed any ideas he had for Victoria. He would never have just written an outline and handed it to her like he would an edict. But this wasn't Marcus she was dealing with anymore. This was Kyle Hunter.

Jeannie toyed with the heavy chain around her neck. She had two choices: give in and take the assignment, knowing that her control of Victoria would be weak at best from then on. Or refuse, knowing Kyle might just let her go. She wouldn't be the first to lose a job at *Aspects* since his return. To make matters worse, no one outside of the office knew she was Victoria Boulderbottom. Any number of people could step in and take over the column. Then what would she do?

A job with another magazine, if she was lucky. Or she could simply pack up and do some traveling again, supporting herself along the way with free-lance work as she'd done so often in the past. But, oddly, the idea held no appeal this time.

She walked purposefully toward his desk. There had to be a way to work this out.

"How about this?" she said brightly. "You run my piece in the next issue and I'll start right away on your series, no arguments. What do you say?"

Kyle ran a hand roughly through his hair. He was beginning to understand what had sent Marcus to Alaska. "I can't believe I'm hearing this. The answer is no." He paused, finally settling on the way to stop her. "Unless..."

"Unless what?"

"You prove 'Marrying Well' works, and I'll print it."

She slumped into the chair across from him. "And how exactly am I supposed to do that?"

"By finding a rich husband, of course."

"That's ridiculous."

"Which is exactly what I've been trying to tell you."

Jeannie got to her feet again, her eyes widening. "But not that ridiculous."

Kyle drew in a deep, calming breath. The woman's mind took more twists than a corkscrew.

"What kind of wealth are we talking?" she asked. "Serious or obscene?"

"Serious will do."

"Old money or new?"

"Either one."

"Legal acquisition only?"

"What do you think?"

A teasing smile touched her lips. "Just asking."

Frustrated that she'd been able to draw him into it again so easily, Kyle got up and rounded the desk. The look of faint surprise that crossed her face changed to curiosity as he reached into his pocket and pulled out a roll of bills. This would put an end to the conversation once and for all.

"No lawsuits pending and strictly North American and you have to do it by Labor Day—that's the deal." He slowly peeled five ten-dollar bills from the roll and dropped them onto the desk. "And fifty bucks says you can't do it." He pushed the money toward her. "What do you say?"

Jeannie looked down at the scattered bills. Kyle had

her and they both knew it. She'd only been playing with possibilities—having fun with the idea. But Kyle had just put everything into a harsh, new light.

Jeannie never refused a dare. Not if she thought she could win at any rate. It all started the day her brother, Pauli, had held a dollar above her head and bet she couldn't sneak into the movie theater without getting caught. No candy had ever tasted as sweet as the one Pauli's money bought for her that afternoon. She'd been hooked ever since.

She shot a quick glance at Kyle. He was watching her closely, measuring her hesitation, judging his chances of winning this one. If she turned him down now, she would be admitting defeat. Then she might as well take his assignment and go home, leaving Victoria firmly in his hands from that point on. The very idea was intolerable.

He arched a brow and smiled at her.

So cocky, Jeannie thought, shifting her attention back to the money. It would serve him right if she called his bluff. After all, it wasn't as though she was in love with anyone at the moment. Or even seeing anyone for that matter. Years of looking, and what did she have to show for it? A string of relationships that had all fizzled within a matter of months.

Maybe it was time to raise her sights. Go for the brass ring. After all, as Aunt Tia used to say, "It's as easy to pick up after a rich one as a poor one." The only question was, could she win?

Jeannie took a step away from the desk. She needed time to think.

"Do you have anything cold in there?" she asked, motioning to the minibar in the corner.

"Just some ice," Kyle replied. "But I could use a drink about now, so why don't I fix us both one. Scotch okay?"

While he tended to glasses and ice, Jeannie made a

quick inventory of everything she would need in order to win.

First, the image had to be perfect: clothes, car—it all had to be right. She already owned a classic 1963 Corvette, inherited from Tia three years ago. Jeannie ticked "car" off her list. Like a string of good pearls, a classic Vette went everywhere.

That still left clothes and a good address. Without hesitation, she ticked them off her list, too. There had to be some room left on one of her credit cards, and if she needed more, she would find it somewhere. She always did. As for the address? She just wouldn't invite him home.

The only thing missing was the man. Jeannie drummed her fingertips on the desk. North America was a big place. It was worth a shot.

Kyle approached with the drinks, a smug smile curving his lips. *Poor Kyle,* Jeannie thought as she accepted the glass. He didn't even know he'd already lost.

"I'm considering your offer," she announced. "But fifty dollars isn't nearly enough."

Kyle reached into his pocket. "How much?"

Jeannie waved a hand. "Put your money away. What I have in mind is much more interesting."

"I'm listening."

Jeannie drained the Scotch, then banged her glass down. "If I take this on, I'll be going out on a limb financially. Projecting the right image alone is going to cost me a fortune. Agreed?"

Kyle nodded and sipped his drink.

"So if I'm successful, you personally will cover all of my expenses. Not the magazine, Kyle. You. Every cent."

"Seems to me that if you win, you'll have more than enough money at your disposal to cover the expenses."

"It's the principle."

"Fair enough. I'll cover the expenses."

Jeannie took a step toward him. "Next, I can see this running as a series now. One installment each week from now until September."

Kyle started to protest but Jeannie held up a hand. "Think about it, Kyle. If you agree to run 'Marrying Well' while I'm out there proving it can be done, the readers can follow Victoria's progress, share in her successes and her failures, but the outcome will be unknown until she actually gets to the end."

He set his drink aside. "Go on," he said casually, but Jeannie saw the spark of interest in his eyes. He was hooked. The time had come to reel him in.

She inched nearer. "Then, after I land a marriage proposal, you make me a partner in the magazine."

"Now wait a minute—"

"I'm not greedy," she interrupted. "Thirty-three percent will be enough."

Kyle's jaw twitched. "I should fire you."

She pushed her lips into a pout as she closed the gap between them. "What's the matter, Kyle? Stakes too high?" She trailed a finger down his chest, deliberately taunting him, inviting him to step back. "Afraid I just might win?"

He glanced down at her hand. "Not for a moment."

"Then what's the problem?" She lazily circled one of his buttons with her fingertip. "The way I figure it, Victoria's readers are going to love watching her hunt down a rich man. The ups, the downs. Will she? Won't she? All of which will mean increased circulation and advertising revenue for you." She grabbed a fistful of his shirt, yanking him forward. "And I want part of that increase."

Kyle gently pried her hand loose and opened her fingers. "That's what I like about you, Jeannie." He pressed his lips to her palm. "You think the way I do."

She let her hand linger in his, surprised as much by

the calluses as the gentleness of his touch. "What exactly are you thinking?"

"What's in it for me, of course."

She tried to pull away but Kyle held firm. "Increased profits and market share," she muttered. "What more do you want?"

He stroked his thumb lightly across hers. "Something that will make it more interesting for me. Something from you. Something personal."

Jeannie stopped struggling. This was unexpected. He smiled and she felt herself melt against him. "Like what?" she murmured, thinking she could change her mind about dimples after all.

Kyle put a finger under her chin and tilted her face up. He lowered his head until she could feel his breath warm on her lips. She waited, her own breath catching in her throat as her mind filled with the scent of Scotch and a million possibilities.

"Like your car," he whispered.

She slapped his hand away. What had she been thinking about? Dimples and warm lips and hard hands and God knows what else. Everything but the business at hand.

"I should have known you'd stoop to this." She clenched her fists as she paced back and forth, annoyed that she'd let her guard down so easily. "Of all the dirty, conniving—"

"I'm conniving? What about you? Thirty-three percent of the magazine?"

"I'll have earned it," she shot back. "Besides, that car has great sentimental value to me."

"What's the matter, Jeannie? Stakes too high? Afraid I just might win?"

She positioned herself safely on the opposite side of the desk and faced him. She didn't wish Kyle any harm for including her Corvette in the wager, only male-pattern baldness—and soon. But it was too late to back down now. She snatched up the bills. "You're on."

While Kyle punched a triumphant fist into the air, Jeannie zipped the money into her pocket. "I'll keep this as an advance."

"And maybe I'll keep your car in my garage."

"Dream on."

"At the very least I should go downstairs and have a look at it. Just to be sure of what I'm getting."

"You're getting a partner, Kyle. Nothing else. Besides, the car's not here. It's in storage until Monday."

"Why? Winter's been over for months."

"Tradition. The Corvette comes out on the first of June. Not a day earlier." She whirled around and headed for the door. "But you could have those share agreements drawn up." She paused with her hand on the knob and smiled at him over her shoulder. "To save time later."

Kyle crossed the room and held the door closed, spoiling her exit. "You really think you can do this, don't you?"

She glanced at his hand then back into his eyes. "You lost our first bet because you underestimated Victoria. And you'll lose this one because you're underestimating me."

2

Jeannie blew Kyle a kiss then spun around, nearly colliding head-on with the woman who had suddenly appeared outside his office door.

He stepped forward to find that Jeannie's hapless victim was LeeAnne Alexander, the woman he had been seeing on and off for the past few weeks.

Kyle reached out to rescue her, but Jeannie's hand was already there, steadying the red-faced beauty.

"I'm so sorry," Jeannie said as LeeAnne regained her footing. "Are you okay?"

"I'm fine," she said, adding a terse, "thank you."

"Let me introduce you a little more formally," Kyle offered. "LeeAnne, this is Jeannie Renamo, one of *Aspects'* writers. Jeannie, this is LeeAnne Alexander."

"Of the Alexander-Haight Gallery," Jeannie finished for him. "I knew I recognized you. You were featured in Magda Ladanski's 'Ladies Who Lunch' series last winter. Something to do with the Mistletoe Charity Ball."

LeeAnne's eyes flicked over Jeannie in quick appraisal. "Among others."

Jeannie extended a hand. "It's nice to meet you."

LeeAnne took hold of her fingertips. "A pleasure."

"Well," Jeannie said, turning her attention to Kyle, "as much as I'd like to stay and chat, I'm afraid I have a lot to do. Places to go, people to meet, that sort of thing." She lowered her lashes. "You understand."

LeeAnne linked her arm through Kyle's as Jeannie headed down the hall. "Well, that certainly was different. Are all of your writers so...interesting?"

"Definitely not," Kyle said, his gaze following the black leather skirt until it disappeared behind one of the partitions. Magda Ladanski's office, he realized and shook his head in admiration. If anyone would know the places to go and the people to meet, it was Magda.

Kyle couldn't help smiling. LeeAnne was on the right track, but "interesting" wasn't quite the right word to describe Jeannie Renamo.

She was a contradiction at every turn. Defiant and mouthy one minute, soft and feminine the next. Even now, he could feel the heat of her hand against his chest, see the spirit in her eyes and the challenge in her smile. But above all, he could hear her startled intake of breath when he lifted her hand and kissed the palm.

He'd expected one of her sharp rebuffs in return for his gesture. Anything but the softening of her spine as she moved against him, seemingly anxious for more of his touch.

A smart maneuver, he gave her that. And one that had almost worked. If not for his own resistance, he could have tasted the Scotch on those lips. And then what?

LeeAnne tugged on his arm. "So, are you going to say hello to me properly, or not?"

Kyle looked down at the woman that common sense told him to hold on to. There was no comparison between her and the one who occupied his thoughts at the moment.

LeeAnne was a slender classic beauty with finely chiseled features and a thick mane of lustrous chestnut hair. Always refined and elegant, her nose didn't wrinkle when she smiled and she certainly didn't throw her head back when she laughed.

But more importantly, LeeAnne didn't argue every blasted little point until he couldn't remember what he had been talking about in the first place. She would fit so easily into the carefully structured life he had made for himself, barely causing the slightest ripple by her presence. And when it was time to for him to leave, she'd slip out again just as easily.

LeeAnne was everything he thought he needed. Yet the longer he studied her, the more Kyle found himself searching for that single flaw that would make her beauty intriguing. And was disappointed to find none.

Pushing the thought aside, Kyle wrapped his arms around LeeAnne and pulled her into his office. "Hello," he whispered, closing the door behind him with his foot.

LeeAnne pressed her body against him and offered her mouth to be kissed. Kyle bent to her, lightly touching his lips to hers, but still finding himself dreaming of another pair of lips—a pair much warmer and fuller than these.

Jeannie stood in the doorway of the cluttered cubicle, staring at the back of the entertainment and social editor's chair. "Magda," she whispered. "Are you busy?"

Magda Ladanski kept the phone pressed to her ear as she swiveled the chair around. The grim expression she wore brightened when she saw who it was.

"Not for you. Come in, come in," she invited, stretching her arm back to drop the receiver on the cradle. The phone-to-the-ear trick and serious expression were for Kyle's benefit, Jeannie knew. "As a matter of fact you're just in time." Yanking open her bottom drawer, she lifted out a small white box tied with string. "Strudel from Henriksson's." She laid the prize before Jeannie. "Still warm."

Magda Ladanski was one of the few people Jeannie

knew who never worried about her weight. She maintained that on the eve of her forty-fifth birthday, the Goddess of Menopause had granted her a lovely black mustache and a license to eat. The mustache Magda was still fighting, but the license she'd embraced with frightening enthusiasm. Usually Jeannie was a willing follower, but for the first time in recent memory, the aroma of apples and cinnamon failed to move her. "Maybe later," she said, then dragged a chair to the desk and sat down. "Right now I have to talk to you."

Magda shrugged and pulled the box back. "So talk."

"I have made either the most brilliant move of my career today, or the blunder of the year."

"Again?"

"Magda, this is serious. I'm getting married."

"Sure. And I'll be the feature model in next year's swimsuit edition." Magda slid the string from the box and lifted the lid, revealing two thick, syrupy slices of apple strudel. "This," she said solemnly, "is what God intended strudel to be."

Jeannie slapped the lid down. "Will you forget the strudel? I'm really getting married."

"And that's the big blunder?" Magda pulled a linen napkin from the drawer and settled it on her lap. "Don't worry so much. Marriage isn't that bad. I've enjoyed all three of mine. Parts of them anyway. Who knows, in a weak moment, I might even do it again." She plucked two silver forks from the pencil holder and set one in front of Jeannie. "We'll eat to your happiness."

Jeannie pushed the fork aside. "Magda, I need your help."

"Okay, write this down. Reception at Carmen's and don't sign anything before the ceremony." She stuck a hand into the middle slot of her message tray and withdrew two china plates. "So who's the lucky guy?"

"I don't know yet."

"Good plan. That way if you change your mind, no one gets hurt." Reaching into the box, Magda carefully lifted the first slice of strudel. "Help me out, here."

Jeannie held up a plate. "You don't understand. I need you to help me find one."

"Find what?"

"A groom, of course."

Magda glanced around. "Did I miss something? Is there a sign in here that says Matchmaker?"

Jeannie lowered her voice to a conspiratorial level. "No, but I think you'll find the role quite interesting once you hear what I have to say."

Magda set her fork down. "I'm listening."

Jeannie briefly outlined what had happened in Kyle's office—the bet, the stakes, everything except one small detail. There was no need to tell anyone she'd actually believed, for even a brief moment, that Kyle Hunter was going to kiss her. Or that she would have let him.

Not that it had been anything more than a momentary lapse. A barrier had been broken when she touched him, and it needed to be rebuilt, that was all.

So why did she still feel so unsettled? Why did the thought of his breath on her lips make her mouth dry and her palms damp?

Too many men and too little sex, she decided. Marriage was just what she needed. And thirty-three percent of the magazine wouldn't hurt, either.

By the time she reached the end of the story, the light in Magda's eyes was so bright, it was almost unholy. Jeannie sat back, knowing she'd come to the right place. "So what do you think?"

Magda slapped both hands on the desk. "I think you're brilliant. I can already picture you sitting in that front office. Personal secretary, big executive chair, the whole bit. But I have to admit I'm surprised that Kyle agreed to the share thing."

"Why do you say that?"

"Because *Aspects* is his baby. Other than his condo, it was the only thing he held on to when he went back to Maine." She shook her head. "I can't see him parting with his shares that easily."

"I don't think he sees me as a serious threat," Jeannie admitted. "And to be honest, I'm beginning to have a few doubts myself."

"This is a first." Magda rocked forward and propped her elbows on the desk. "Aren't you the same woman who ran off to join the circus, just to prove that she hadn't yet met all the clowns in the world?"

"This is different," Jeannie insisted. "We're not just talking a beer with the boys anymore. We're talking marriage. As in forever."

"Not necessarily."

Jeannie shook her head solemnly. "For me it has to be. At least I have to go in believing it will be." She stood up to wander around the tiny office. "Why do you think I've never married before now?"

"Nobody's asked you?"

"Very cute."

Magda shrugged. "It's a natural conclusion. In all the time I've known you, you've never once been serious about a man." She pointed a finger at her. "As a matter of fact, I think the reason you've never married is because you're afraid."

"I'm not afraid." Jeannie flopped into the chair again. "I'm careful."

Magda pursed her lips and considered. "You say you want forever," she said at length. "But I think the idea scares you to death. That's why Victoria Boulderbottom works so well for you. She lets you have the fun of looking, yet allows you to keep this nice, professional distance from every man you meet. They're all strictly research material to you. Men under a microscope, so to speak.''

"You're wrong. I've just never met the right man.''

"And so you assume you won't find him this time, either. Is that it? Just because a man is rich, he can't be lovable. Is that what you're saying?''

Jeannie pushed herself out of the chair. "Now you're putting words in my mouth. I'm just worried about what will happen if I don't find the right one this time, either. I can't marry someone just to win a bet. But if I don't get married, I lose my aunt Tia's Corvette.'' She winced at the thought. "She'll come back and haunt me—I know it.''

"So if you lose, you pay Kyle the value of the car. No big deal.''

"For you maybe,'' Jeannie muttered and slumped into the chair. "I don't have that kind of money.''

"Then make up your mind you're going to win. For the next little while, every time you meet a man, keep your mind and your heart open. Who knows? Maybe one of them will turn out to be Mr. Right. Then when he asks you to marry him, you won't run away. Agreed?''

Jeannie studied her friend's earnest face. For Magda, there was a simple solution to everything. You're looking for strudel—you keep your nose open. You're looking for love—you keep your heart open. No big deal.

"Agreed?'' Magda prompted again.

Jeannie knew that arguing with Magda was like using a treadmill: you went on and on and still ended up at the same place. But maybe she had a point.

The perfect man might be sitting inside his limousine right now, champagne on ice and heart in hand, just waiting to give it all to a woman with red hair and big hips. Stranger things had happened.

Jeannie smiled at her. "Agreed.''

Magda thumped a fist on the desk. "Good. Now, how

can I help you? One way or another, you have to win. I can't bear the thought of never having another ride in that car of yours.''

"Give me a place to start," Jeannie suggested. "You deal with celebrities every day. I thought you could introduce me to a few. Let me get my feet wet."

"You don't want a Hollywood type," Magda said with conviction. "Too flighty." She stood and yanked open the top drawer of her filing cabinet. "What you need is a rich man who prefers a low profile. More stability and fewer groupies." She rifled through the files. "Not old money, but money that's been around long enough to earn a little interest. Here we go." She pulled out a folder and laid it down in front of Jeannie. "This should give you exactly what you need."

Jeannie read the label. "Upcoming Social Events?"

"Precisely." Magda flipped back the cover and spread the contents across the desk. "Gallery openings, fundraisers, all kinds of things. Deadly dull affairs for the most part, but always crawling with rich men."

Jeannie thumbed through the cards, feeling any lingering doubts fade as her own excitement began to build. "This is wonderful. Anything coming up soon?"

Magda poked through the pile. "As a matter of fact, there's a big gala tonight." She pulled a pale pink card from the stack and dangled it in front of Jeannie's face. "This is it. 'Antique Market Gala.' Westfield Inn, seven o'clock. Over six hundred members of the horsey set will be there sipping champagne and nibbling caviar. I was going to stop in on my way to the opening of a new show. If you want, you can go in my place."

Jeannie snapped the invitation out of her hand and headed for the door. "I'll let you know how it goes."

"Hold on a minute, Cinderella. You're not ready to go to the ball yet." Magda gave her Rolodex a spin. "Don't take this the wrong way, dear, but that little leather number you're wearing really won't be appropriate.''

Jeannie touched a hand to her chest. ''I'm wounded.''

''You'll get over it.'' Magda walked her fingers across the top of the cards, pulled one and tossed it to Jeannie. ''Lissa Stiller. She's a designer. New, but very good. I've featured her a few times in my column. Tell her I sent you and then tell her you're Victoria Boulderbottom. She reads you all the time. Maybe she'll give you a break.''

Jeannie examined the card. ''And maybe she'll lend me a few dresses for free.''

''Dream on.''

''Think about it. If I promise to wear only her designs while I'm doing this and give her extensive coverage in my column, she might just go for it.''

Magda's eyes widened. ''You are the most devious woman I know.''

Jeannie smiled. ''That's why we get along so well.''

Magda gathered her jacket around her and perched on the corner of the desk. ''I'll speak to her first if you like.''

''No thanks.'' Jeannie picked up a pen and scribbled Lissa's name and phone number onto the back of the invitation. ''I'd rather not give her too much advance notice.'' She handed the card back to Magda. ''Thanks for everything. I owe you.''

''You sure do.'' Magda reached for her slice of strudel. ''But for now, all I ask is that you remember your promise.''

Jeannie picked up the forks and held Magda's out to her. ''Open mind, open heart,'' she said with fake solemnity.

''Go ahead, laugh. This might just work.''

Jeannie reached into the box, lifted out the other slice of strudel and plunked it on a plate. ''To marriage,'' she said, hoisting it into the air.

Magda raised her strudel in reply. ''To love.''

* * *

"Is something wrong?" LeeAnne murmured.

Kyle released her and stepped back. "Of course not. Why do you ask?"

She gave her head a single, refined shake. "You seem preoccupied, that's all."

"I've got a lot on my mind."

LeeAnne took hold of his hand and led him to the sofa by the credenza. "Which is exactly why I'm here." She sat down and patted the seat next to her. "I'm on my way to the Westfield to check the final arrangements for the opening of the Antique Market tonight. I thought I might be able to talk you into coming with me."

"I don't think so, LeeAnne."

"But I've arranged a special Victorian tea for the committee." She laced her fingers with his and tried to pull him down. "I know you'll love it."

Kyle withdrew his hand and returned to his desk. "Maybe so, but I can't leave right now."

"Of course." LeeAnne stood and walked to the credenza, then turned to him, the faintest trace of a smile curving her lips. "And while I'm disappointed, I do understand."

As always. Kyle fought to suppress a smile as an image of Jeannie standing in the same spot came to mind: hip thrust forward defiantly, mouth in action as usual. She would never be understanding or predictable. If anything, she would be an exhausting experience. Too much energy, too much will, too much everything. But interesting.

"Did you hear what I said?"

Kyle looked up to find LeeAnne standing directly in front of him.

"I asked if you've reconsidered going to the gala tonight."

When he didn't answer, she lifted a graceful wrist and

checked her watch. "You have the invitation if you do. I have to run."

"That's fine." He walked her to the door, surprised that the idea of being free of her should appeal to him so much.

He opened the door in time to see Jeannie backing out of Magda's office, brandishing a piece of paper as though it were a sword. Her face was flushed, her smile broad as she turned and caught him watching her.

She didn't miss a beat, simply flicked the page as though thumbing her nose at him, then whirled around and sashayed down the hall, hips rolling seductively with each exaggerated step. The gauntlet had been dropped.

"Can you believe that?" LeeAnne whispered.

Kyle took hold of her arm and propelled her down the hall. "Yes, LeeAnne. I can. She honestly believes she's going to win."

"Win what?"

"Never mind." He stopped outside Magda's office. "I hope the tea goes well," he said hastily, and left LeeAnne standing in the hall.

Magda spun her chair around as he entered. Kyle took the phone out of her hand and hung it up. "Make sure there's a line lit up next time."

Magda laughed and held out a box of chocolates. "I never could fool you. Have one."

"No thanks." He leaned both hands on her desk. "I want to know what you gave to Jeannie Renamo."

Magda selected a chocolate and popped it into her mouth. "I don't know what you're talking about."

Kyle smiled. "Magda, how would you like to spend a month covering dog shows?"

Her hand froze over the box. "You wouldn't."

He cocked an eyebrow in reply.

"All right, all right. I gave her an invitation to the 'Antique Market Gala' tonight."

"What else?"

She popped in another chocolate. "Nothing."

"We could include in-depth coverage of bowling banquets, too."

Magda started to cough. "The name of a designer," she said, gasping. "That's all. I swear."

"Which designer?"

She held out the card.

"Lissa Stiller," he read, then thumped Magda firmly on the back. "Thanks, Magda. You're a sport."

She drew in a deep breath. "Please don't tell her I told you anything."

He headed for the door. "Not as long as you keep me informed every time she takes an invitation from that file of yours."

Kyle walked back to his office, a curious lightness settling over him. His eyes were drawn to the disk he had given Jeannie earlier. He picked it up and turned it over in his hand. Had it been purposely ignored or simply forgotten? With Jeannie Renamo, who could tell.

Not that it mattered, he thought as he dropped it into his pocket. He would return it to her tonight.

3

Just an hour's drive north of the city, the Westfield Inn appealed to those who preferred a slower pace, attention to detail and a soothing, clublike atmosphere. Uniformed bellboys still carried messages on silver trays, tea was served each day at precisely four o'clock and dinner was generally followed by a stroll through the gardens.

On the surface, everything about the refurbished estate home was old-fashioned charm, while behind the scenes, computers, fax machines and a dedicated staff made certain that the Westfield kept pace with the competition, providing all the amenities a modern traveler or convention planner required.

With over five acres of manicured grounds, stained-glass windows and vaulted ceilings, the Westfield provided a mood of quiet Victorian elegance, making it the perfect setting for the Antique Market.

Opening night was traditionally a gala affair for charity, and entrance was by invitation only. The evening was set to begin at seven o'clock with a special preview of the exhibits in the Grand Ballroom, followed by dinner and dancing in the smaller but equally lavish Green and Gold Room.

By six-thirty, the salon outside the ballroom was alive with conversation and laughter. Sequins and taffeta shimmered in the glow of crystal chandeliers, a four-piece chamber orchestra performed Vivaldi's *Four Seasons* and white-gloved waiters circulated with trays of champagne and hors d'oeuvres while the city's elite waited patiently for the doors to open.

Jeannie stood alone on the sidelines, scanning the crowd while she drained her second glass of champagne. So far, the only thing that had gone right that day was her meeting with Lissa Stiller.

The designer had taken to Jeannie's suggestion immediately, and the two women had spent the afternoon selecting an appropriate wardrobe for Victoria's quest, including the dress Jeannie had chosen for the gala: a simple poppy-red shift in a delicate silk crepe that skimmed over her body like a lover's touch.

She had never worn anything like it, and only hoped it wouldn't be considered too formal if she decided to drop into her favorite club later. While there probably wouldn't be any limos parked out front, there would definitely be some single men parked inside. Which was more than she could say for the Westfield.

Jeannie perked up as another group entered, then let her shoulders slump again. "Nothing but couples," she muttered and slapped her glass on the table beside her.

"What did you expect?" a male voice whispered in her ear.

She whirled around, a bright smile already in place. "Oh, I don't know—" She stopped abruptly, dropping the smile when she realized the blue eyes she was gazing into belonged to Kyle Hunter. "What are you doing here?"

"I was invited."

"I'd forgotten that LeeAnne Alexander is the gala chair. I should have known you'd be here."

He merely smiled. "And you?"

"I'm not crashing, if that's what you think." Jeannie

turned away, making up her mind to ignore him, knowing it was already too late.

In a sea of predictable tux and bow-tie combinations, Kyle Hunter still managed to stand out. The formal lines of the jacket suited him, emphasizing the width of his shoulders and the straight line of his back, the gloss of refinement only enhancing a masculinity Jeannie already found overwhelming.

The ballroom doors swung open and the crowd surged forward.

"If you'll excuse me."

She moved off, intending to join the line when Kyle's hand closed on her arm, gently but firmly holding her in place. "Why not wait until the rush is over?"

Nabbing a glass of champagne from a passing waiter, he shifted his hold at the same time, making it look as though she were a willing companion. Very subtle. Very shrewd. Very frustrating.

"But that's part of the fun," she protested, fighting the urge to let herself enjoy the warmth of his hand on her bare skin while reminding herself that distance was the key.

He sipped thoughtfully. "You find these affairs fun?"

"I don't know yet. I've never been to one."

"What do you think so far?"

Ignoring her own warnings, Jeannie relaxed against him while she considered. "There is a certain allure, I suppose. But I have to admit I haven't seen so many black outfits since the last biker party I went to."

The shift in his stance was so slight, it would have gone unnoticed had she not been standing so close. "You go to biker parties?"

Jeannie smiled up at him. "Only once. I was doing some preliminary research for a series I was going to call 'Hawg Wild.' Someone told me they meet in Port Dover every Friday the thirteenth, so I went."

"Alone?"

"Of course."

His tone became less affable. "And Marcus allowed this?"

"He couldn't have stopped me."

Kyle's eyes darkened as he turned to face her. "I would have."

She could find nothing mocking in his tone or his expression. Just a genuine concern she found disarming. "You might have tried," she said gently. "But I'm afraid I don't take orders very well."

"So I've noticed."

Touching a hand to his, Jeannie gently withdrew the delicate champagne flute from his fingers. "You're going to break this if you're not careful."

Kyle cursed himself for having been so obvious, but couldn't resist watching as she raised his glass to her lips, her eyes teasing him over the rim. As quickly as it had come, his annoyance began to fade, only to be replaced by a sudden desire to kiss her.

Not slowly or tenderly, but hard and deep. Making her bend to his will until the knowing light in her eyes was gone and her body melted against his as it had that morning. Which wasn't the reason he was there.

It would be some other man's job to teach this one to take orders, not his. He was only there to watch and feel sorry for whomever it was she chose. And to make sure she had his assignment with her when she left.

"Shall we go inside?" Kyle offered his arm and was only a little surprised when she set the glass down and looped her arm over his. To expect the unexpected was the only way to deal with Jeannie Renamo. "You still haven't told me what brings you here."

She grinned at him. "A keen interest in antiques."

"Or a keen interest in a finding a husband?"

"That, too," she conceded on a whispered note of laughter.

She moved closer as they joined the line, and Kyle caught the delicate scent of her perfume. A light, feminine floral he would have said was all wrong for her, but was somehow exactly right.

Annoyed with himself for drifting again, Kyle concentrated on the crowd instead. "So you think this will be the place to find one?"

Jeannie sighed. "I had hoped it would be a start. But I have to admit, the pickings look a little slim."

"Well, things may be looking up. Here comes a single one now."

She followed his gaze to the entrance. A man stood motionless as he eyed the line, then he raised a hand in greeting and came toward them at a leisurely pace, pausing often to speak to someone or shake a hand.

"It's like watching a royal walkabout," Jeannie remarked.

"Crown Prince Duncan Fox," Kyle murmured.

"Is he rich?"

"Filthy."

"What does he do?"

"Nothing." Kyle looked down at her. "But don't worry. Duncan may not be the working kind, but he's definitely the marrying kind. Been through two wives already. Maybe I could set you up."

She broke away. "Kyle, if you say a word—"

"Trust me," he whispered as the man drew nearer.

Right. Like the spider and the fly, Jeannie thought and gave serious consideration to slipping away until Kyle snaked an arm around her waist, effectively eliminating the possibility.

"Just relax," he murmured as Duncan stepped up beside them.

Jeannie was about to protest when Duncan turned his

smile on her. It was a smile that said, "Hello. You're beautiful. So am I. And if you stay, I'm sure you'll find that's not all we have in common."

Since Jeannie had always been fond of eloquent smiles, she took Kyle's advice. She relaxed.

"Kyle," Duncan said. "It's been a long time."

Kyle shook his hand. "Yes it has."

Duncan was as tall as Kyle but his build was leaner, bordering on thin. He sported a navy tuxedo jacket and striped pants—an interesting choice, Jeannie thought. The bow tie had been abandoned in favour of an ice blue shirt with a banded collar, worn open of course, and a deep-cut, white vest.

His dark hair was swept back from his face and she was sure he hadn't bothered to shave. The total effect was devastating—sophisticated and urbane with an element of danger. But perhaps just a little studied, a little too perfect to be natural. Maybe if he'd just stop smiling for a while—

You're doing it, Jeannie reminded herself. *Finding reasons to write him off before you're even introduced.*

"I heard you were in town again," Duncan was saying. "Been meaning to call. Will you be staying long?"

"I hope not."

"So the charms of city life are nothing compared to the lure of wood slivers—is that it?" Duncan asked.

"Wood slivers have very little to do with it."

"I suppose not." Duncan turned to Jeannie, the ever-present smile broadening to a grin as his gaze skimmed over her. "And who is this?"

Open heart, open mind, she chanted silently, and turned up the radiance of her smile to match Duncan's as Kyle drew her forward.

"Duncan Fox, I'd like you to meet Jeannie Renamo. She's here doing some…"

Jeannie sent him a warning glance.

"Research?" he said at last.

"Really." Duncan moved a step closer and extended a hand to her. "What kind of research?"

"Victoriana," she said in the voice she saved for special occasions. She took his hand, holding on a moment longer than necessary while she let her gaze sweep over him slowly and deliberately, making certain she missed nothing. The deep breath he took told her he approved.

"Yes," Kyle added. "Jeannie is especially interested in the social mores of the period. You know. Love, marriage. Traditions, marriage. Class distinctions, marriage—"

"Kyle," she purred.

He raised his brows in question. "Yes, Jeannie?" That innocent expression didn't fool her. He knew exactly what he was doing. And he was enjoying it—a very bad sign. What she needed now was a graceful exit before he could do any real damage.

"I'm sure Duncan isn't interested in the details of my research," she said, keeping her tone so sweet, she hoped Kyle would choke on it. "Besides, you two probably have a lot to catch up on. So if you gentlemen will excuse me."

She shot Duncan one last glance, trying to make it significant but not obvious. She'd done everything but drool on his shoes to let him know she was interested. The next move was definitely up to him.

"It's been a pleasure," she murmured, then headed into the ballroom.

When she was well out of earshot, Duncan turned to Kyle. "Let's cut this short, shall we? What's your stake in Jeannie Renamo?"

"None whatsoever," Kyle said and forced a smile. "Be my guest."

"That's great." Duncan checked his watch. "I'll give her an hour or so to wonder. That should be long enough." He lifted his head. "Been great talking to you, Kyle, and thanks."

"No problem," Kyle told him, and headed for the ball-room.

Jeannie wandered through the rows of antiques, check-ing for signs of single men and catching fragments of conversation along the way. After a while, she ended the search for men and gave herself over completely to eavesdropping, never failing to be amazed by the amount of money people were willing to pay for butterflies, brass candlesticks and photographs of dour-faced men and women.

She lifted a hand-painted teacup, the color of a robin's egg and just as delicate, holding the tiny handle gingerly between her fingers. The cup was lovely, and probably worth every penny the dealer was asking, but Jeannie had no desire to bring the past into her present. No matter how hard she tried, she simply couldn't understand the glow of romance that surrounded the past.

As far as she was concerned, the past was a time when most women lived out their lives in the shadows, trading their independence for the security of marriage and the protection of a man; becoming just another part of his property. Mrs. John Doe. No name. No dreams. Just a cupboard full of dainty china cups that needed washing.

Deciding to call it a night, Jeannie set the cup down and stepped out into the aisle again. She was on her way to the exit when a booth called Old Mistresses caught her eye.

Curious, Jeannie took a few steps closer. As she ap-proached, an elderly woman rose from a folding chair. Her face was heavily lined, her white hair sparse, but the smile she beamed at Jeannie was one of real pleasure, and her eyes were those of a woman young in spirit.

"Come in," she beckoned. "It's been so slow down

this end, I was almost falling asleep.'' She offered her hand. ''I'm Ellie Jacobs. Welcome to Old Mistresses.''

Jeannie smiled. ''Old Mistresses.''

''As opposed to Old Masters,'' Ellie replied, her voice as clear as her handshake was firm. ''What you see here is the art of women. Take your time. Have a good look around.''

Jeannie moved from one display to another, admiring the paintings and intricate pen-work pieces, but it was a simple photograph that made her stop. Set in a heavy gilt frame, the shot was of a young woman and handsome officer standing by a garden wall, remarkable only because there was nothing at all dour about the woman's expression.

Her hair was down and blowing in the wind, her chin lifted and her smile broad; she was actually laughing. The soldier, on the other hand, frowned deeply, apparently displeased with her. Jeannie liked her immediately.

''A fascinating picture,'' a male voice whispered behind her.

Jeannie turned, coming face to chest with Duncan Fox.

''You scared me half to death,'' she scolded playfully as she backed up.

''I didn't mean to.'' He leaned down to whisper in her ear. ''It's just that I couldn't stop thinking about you.''

Then what took you so long, she thought, but bit back the remark. ''Really?'' was the only safe reply that came to mind.

He nodded. ''Unfortunately, Kyle tied me up for the longest time. He can be like that, you know.''

No, she didn't. The Kyle she knew was generally a man of few words, but obviously Duncan knew a different Kyle Hunter. ''I'll take your word for it.''

Duncan ran a finger up and down her arm. ''I usually don't mind, but tonight the only thing on my mind was

finding the beautiful woman who captured my heart the
moment I saw her.''

Oh, please, Jeannie thought, biting her lip as she
fought to keep her smile in place.

Duncan laughed softly. ''I have to tell you, Jeannie,
I'm usually a pretty good judge of character, but you had
me completely fooled. I never dreamed you'd be the type
to go all tongue-tied and trembly.'' He hushed her pro-
tests with a fingertip to her lips. ''Don't worry. I like it.''

Only the sound of Ellie Jacobs's voice saved him. ''If
you two have any questions, I'll be right up front.''

Duncan focused his charm on the owner of the booth.
''I only caught the tail end of what you were telling Jeannie. Perhaps you could take a moment and go over it for
me.''

Ellie's face crinkled with delight. ''Let me show you
around personally.''

Jeannie rolled her eyes as Duncan was led away.
Tongue-tied and trembly. She'd have to remember to include that in her next ''Ten Dumbest Things Men Say''
list. Right now, it was in the number-one spot.

Ellie's laughter drifted up from the back of the booth.
Duncan had linked her arm with his and was patting her
hand solicitously. Ellie was actually blushing.

Jeannie turned her attention back to the photograph.
The young woman was lovely and vital, so full of energy
that even the limited photographic equipment of the time
had managed to capture it. From the look on her face,
Jeannie doubted that the woman would be as easily
conned as Ellie Jacobs, and she found herself wondering
what had happened to the couple.

A crooked finger tapped on the frame. ''This was taken
by my mother,'' Ellie said, her pride evident in her tone.
''Most of her work has been lost over the years, but I
managed to salvage a few. This one is my favorite.''

''Who are they?'' Jeannie asked.

"My mother would never tell me," Ellie admitted.

"Such a pity." Duncan moved in to stand next Jeannie. "It would have been nice to know what happened to them."

Jeannie frowned. Although he was echoing her own thoughts, the flat expression in his eyes told her he was not sincere.

She gave him her warmest smile. "With any luck, he went off to war and got killed."

"No," Ellie said, missing Duncan's puzzled expression completely as she turned to gaze at the picture. "From what I gathered, they were engaged to be married. The wedding was to take place a few days after this photograph was taken, but he called the whole thing off quite suddenly." She chuckled. "Caused quite a scandal, I understand."

"I can imagine." On impulse, Jeannie asked, "Is it for sale?"

"It was until about half an hour ago. Sorry."

"Figures," Jeannie muttered. There hung the only piece of history she'd ever wanted, and it was already gone.

Fully recovered, Duncan stepped behind Jeannie and whispered in her ear. "Maybe you'll find something you like in the display of Victorian jewelry farther along the aisle. It's a fascinating collection of botanical creations."

She turned around slowly. "Did you read that somewhere or did you make it up yourself?"

"I read it in their leaflet," he admitted and flashed her a wonderful, boyish grin. "I can read the whole thing to you if you'd like." The smile dimmed ever so slightly. "And maybe I can start over again."

Jeannie studied him a moment. Maybe there was hope.

"Because I'd hate to think you wouldn't sleep with me just because I put my foot in my mouth earlier."

And maybe not.

"Only kidding," he whispered and took her hand. "Come on. I'll buy you a drink."

"Open heart, open mind," she chanted silently, then cast one last look at the laughing face of the woman in the picture as Duncan led her out of the booth.

4

Kyle sat at the back of the Green and Gold Room, watching as waiters hurried to clear the dinner dishes from the surrounding tables. Business was brisk at each of the four bars, the laughter raucous and the dance floor nicely crowded. Although only a few hours old, this year's gala was already proving to be an unparalleled success, and a glowing tribute to LeeAnne Alexander.

She stood talking with a photographer at the front of the room, the sequins on her dress shimmering like black diamonds with every movement.

Beside him, Elliot Daniels followed his gaze, his heavy-lidded eyes seeming to droop even farther than usual. "LeeAnne certainly is a lovely woman."

Kyle smiled at the man who had been his closest friend for over ten years. Elliot hadn't changed much in all that time—still the same hangdog expression and unassuming manner that was so rare in a man of his wealth and position. And of all the people Kyle knew in Chicago, Elliot was the only one he'd been happy to run into at the gala. He turned his attention to the dais again. "Yes, she is," Kyle agreed.

"Smart. Successful. Beautiful."

"Very beautiful."

"But she's not the one, is she."

It was a statement not a question, and Kyle looked at him quizzically. "What makes you say that?"

"Just seeing you together."

"You mean tonight?" Kyle laughed. "That's not too much to go on, considering how busy she's been."

"Exactly." Elliot sat back. "I know you, Kyle. If LeeAnne was the one, you'd have found a way to be with her, regardless of the circumstances."

Irritation prickled the back of Kyle's neck, but he managed to keep his tone light. "That's ridiculous. You know I hate these affairs. Why would I be here if not for her?"

"Because there's something here that you do want." Elliot grinned at him. "And when I figure out what it is, I'll let you know."

Kyle's smile strained. "You're imagining things."

"Maybe," Elliot allowed, but a note of doubt still lingered.

Annoyed, Kyle shifted his attention to the dance floor. He knew he'd been distracted all evening, his mind drifting to *Aspects,* to Bristol Harbor. And always back to Jeannie.

A simple flash of red or a note of distant laughter would have him searching for her, remembering the way she'd looked in that dress, how she'd flirted so outrageously with Duncan and wondering if he'd found her yet.

Nothing more than natural curiosity, he'd assured himself over and over again. And understandable since he had a vested interest in the outcome. But it wasn't something he was ready to discuss with anyone. Not even Elliot.

As the orchestra eased into their own mellow version of a Rolling Stones tune, he turned back to Elliot, hoping to sidetrack him once and for all. "I could use a change of pace. Want to try the bar downstairs?"

Elliot lifted a brow. "You buying?"

"Naturally."

"Then I'm with you." Elliot stood up and followed him to the door. "At least we know the music can't be any worse."

"Have you thought any more about joining us for Race Week?" Kyle asked as they stepped onto the escalator. "We could really use you on the crew, Elliot."

Elliot shrugged. "No reason not to, is there?" His smile was a sorry effort. "It's not like there's anyone around to miss me."

Kyle silently cursed himself as they crossed the granite floor. He hadn't meant to open that wound, only to keep the focus away from himself and LeeAnne. "You still haven't heard from Yvonne, have you?" he asked softly.

"Not a word in six months. I'm okay with it now though. Really."

But Kyle saw the lie in his eyes. "She's going through with the divorce, then?"

"That's what my lawyer tells me." Elliot squared his shoulders and tried to shake the sadness off. "But that's water under the bridge, so if you want me for Race Week, I'm all yours."

Kyle clapped him on the shoulder. "That's great. I'll call Bristol Harbor first thing in the morning and let everyone know. It's about time you started getting out more, dating a little."

Elliot looked skeptical. "I haven't dated in years."

"Then Race Week will be perfect. Sailing all day, parties all night. Believe me, we'll have a great time."

Elliot's smile was real this time. "Maybe we'll even come up with a name for that boat of yours."

Kyle opened the door to the Westfield's Lionhead Lounge. "I wouldn't count on it. Besides, I'm sort of used to calling her *The Boat* now."

The two men stepped into the bar, hesitating a moment as they grew accustomed to the dim lighting. Modeled after a Victorian gentlemen's club, the Lionhead was a place of deep, comfortable chairs and dark wood paneling, where unobtrusive waiters whisked away empty glasses and delivered refills beneath dark-toned oil paintings.

As Kyle scanned the room for an empty table, a couple seated at a corner banquette caught his eye. The woman crossed and uncrossed her long legs while her fingers tapped the stem of her wineglass. Even in such shadowy light, there was no mistaking the restlessness of her movements or the graceful curve of her legs. It was Jeannie. And the man across from her was Duncan.

"There's a spot over there," Elliot said, pointing in the opposite direction.

"Hold on." Kyle took a few steps in her direction, merely to satisfy his curiosity, of course, but stopped abruptly when Duncan reached under the table and trailed a lazy finger along her calf.

"Is that Duncan Fox?" Elliot asked.

Kyle's gaze fixed on Duncan's hand. "None other," he mumbled, relaxing only slightly when Jeannie plucked the wandering appendage from her leg and dropped it on the table.

He half expected her to get up and leave, but she didn't. And why would she? Whatever else Duncan might be, he was also rich and available—the only two things she needed in a man right now, thanks to their bet.

"You know," Elliot said wistfully. "I've always told myself I wouldn't want Duncan's life. One shallow relationship after another. But I have to admit I could go for shallow about now. Especially if it looked like her."

"Well he's wasting his time with this one," Kyle assured him.

"You know her?"

"Her name is Jeannie Renamo. She works at *Aspects*." Kyle consciously relaxed his stance even as he watched

Duncan lift Jeannie's hand to his lips and kiss her fingertips. "Let's go find that table."

Elliot turned to follow, but reluctantly. "Okay. I guess we know how it's going to turn out anyway."

Kyle froze. "Meaning?"

"Meaning that Duncan's obviously got plans for this Jeannie of yours." He looked back over his shoulder. "And knowing Duncan, he'll get exactly what he wants."

Something sudden and bitter and out of all proportion to the casual remark twisted inside Kyle. Anger? Jealousy? He immediately rejected both. "She's not my Jeannie," he said evenly. "She's an employee." And as long as it didn't end in a marriage proposal, what happened between her and Duncan was no concern of his.

As he was turning away, he noticed Duncan leaning closer to say something to Jeannie. Abruptly she jerked her hand back and slid to the end of the banquette. She was just flipping the slender purse strap over her shoulder when she caught sight of him standing a few tables away.

Kyle watched, fascinated, as her eyes widened and her mouth rounded to a soft O. He raised a questioning brow and her mouth snapped shut. In one smooth movement, she dropped the purse and swung her legs around, making a show of lacing her fingers with Duncan's as she slid back across the seat.

Saving face, Kyle thought, and the bitterness began to fade, replaced by a sense of relief so strong, he couldn't stop a broad grin from stretching across his face. He'd known all along that Duncan wouldn't be the one.

"I thought he'd lost her for a moment," Elliot said.

"He did."

"I don't know. She still looks pretty friendly."

She was trying, Kyle gave her that. Laughing, smiling, her gaze fixed on Duncan as though his every word captivated her. But her movements were forced, unnatural.

"No," Kyle said softly. "She's not friendly at all. Just watch her hands. She may be letting him hold one, but the other's gripping that wineglass as though it was a lifeline." He smiled at Elliot. "Trust me. She's furious."

Elliot eyed him curiously. "How well do you know this woman?"

"Hardly at all." Kyle looked back at her. "I told you, she's an employee." A beautiful, stubborn employee who was about to lose the biggest bet of her life. He smiled at Elliot. "How about that drink?"

Jeannie tossed her hair in what she hoped was a casual manner and tried to catch a quick glimpse over her shoulder at the same time, hoping Kyle would be gone. But he was still there, toasting her from a table in the corner.

She turned back as Duncan moved around to her side of the banquette.

"You really had me fooled," he told her. "For a moment, I actually thought you were going to leave." Chuckling, he stroked his thumb across hers. "I'm sorry if I came on a little strong. It's just that you're so damned exciting."

He touched his lips to the side of her neck and Jeannie snapped her shoulder up. "Please don't do that."

He gave her a sly, knowing grin. "Makes you crazy, huh?"

"You don't know the half of it," Jeannie muttered, lifting her wineglass, and knowing she couldn't continue this much longer.

By rights she should have left hours ago, about the same time her mind had shut down for the night. But had she gone? Of course not. She'd held on, keeping her heart open a crack, just in case. She smacked the glass down onto the table. Served her right for not following her own judgment in the first place.

Duncan nuzzled his face in her hair. "Let's stop kidding around. Why deny ourselves any longer?"

"Trust me, Duncan," she grunted as she shoved him back. "I'm not denying myself a thing."

He sat back smiling. "You can't fool me. You're as hot for me as I am for you." He raised his glass in salute. "Bottoms up. And soon."

Enough was enough. Better to endure Kyle's laughter than waste any more time with Prince Duncan. "Good night." She slipped her purse over her shoulder and stood up. "It's been lovely."

Duncan's drink slopped over his hand as he hurried to his feet. "Wait," he ordered, shaking the drops onto the carpet. "I've got something to show you."

He reached into his pocket and pulled out a key. "Room 112," he whispered, then took her hand and placed the key into her palm. "Everything is there. Chilled wine, plump strawberries and warm, melted chocolate. What do you say?"

Jeannie looked down at the key. "Nice idea, but strawberries give me a rash."

His smile faltered. "You're telling me no?"

"You catch on quick." She held out the key. "Good night, Duncan."

"I don't believe this. Do you have any idea how many women would kill to have that key in their hand?"

"Hundreds, I'm sure."

"Damn right."

"Then you'll have no trouble getting rid of this." Jeannie laid the key on the table. "I really have to go."

He grabbed her arm. "Women don't normally tell me no, Jeannie."

In one swift move, she broke the hold and stepped back. "Then this will be a new experience for you, won't it?"

"Wait," he called after her, but she kept going, pausing only briefly when she reached the door. She glanced over at Kyle's table, her spirits rising when she saw that he was turned the other way, evidently locked in a conversation with his friend. With a little luck, she could get out before he even knew she was gone.

Stepping into the bright lights of the lobby, Jeannie stopped long enough to decide her next move. Drawn by the promise of fresh air and open space, Jeannie straightened her shoulders and headed for the terrace.

Declining a waiter's offer to find her a table on the terrace, Jeannie continued down the flagstone steps to the walkways and gardens beyond.

The trees lining the paths were decorated with thousands of tiny white lights, lending a fairy-tale quality to the evening. Once away from the crush, Jeannie slowed her pace, taking time to admire the lighted statuary along the winding paths, and letting the scent of lilacs and wildflowers fill her head.

She stopped by a low stone wall, enjoying the way the breeze moved through her hair and raised tiny goose bumps on her arms. Music, soft and hazy as a dream, drifted down from the ballroom. With a contented sigh, Jeannie settled into the corner of a wrought-iron bench. This, she decided as she closed her eyes, was her reward for endurance.

Kyle who had discreetly followed her from the bar, watched her from a distance and waited. The run-in with Duncan hadn't left her upset or shaken at all. If anything, she looked completely relaxed and peaceful, as though it were all just part of a day.

Maybe it was, he mused. She was, after all, Victoria Boulderbottom's foot soldier. A woman who took dares and went to biker parties and was far too independent for her own good.

Looking at her now, though, it was hard to see her that way. With her face bathed in pale moonlight, she seemed softer somehow—almost the way she'd looked in his office that morning when he'd come so close to kissing her.

Knowing it was best to leave that memory alone and content that she was safe, he turned to leave.

"Good night, Kyle."

His head snapped around at the sound of her voice. She was facing him now, arms folded, legs crossed and chin lifted high. Staying a step ahead of Jeannie Renamo was definitely going to be a challenge. He strolled toward her. "If you knew I was here, why didn't you say something?"

"Because I wanted to see how long you'd stand there." She rested one arm on the back of the bench, her fingers absently stroking the petals of an iron flower while she studied him. "I suppose you saw what happened in the bar?"

"It was hard not to."

"And you've come to gloat."

"I came to make sure you were all right."

She eyed him warily as he sat down beside her. "Why?"

"Because you left in such a hurry. I couldn't hear what was said, but I imagine it wasn't, 'Let's have coffee.'"

Her shoulders relaxed as she angled her body toward him. "Actually, it was strawberries."

"Ah, yes. The old strawberries-and-chocolate routine," he said, feeling an absurd jolt of pleasure when a smile curved her lips.

"Sounds like you know him well."

"We were friends in college."

She cocked her head to the side. "That surprises me."

Kyle shrugged. "We each had something the other wanted, so it suited our needs for a while."

"I'm trying to imagine what Duncan could possibly have offered you, but I'm coming up empty."

"Try money."

He watched her eyes, knowing she wanted to know more but waiting to see how far she would push. Wisely, she changed the subject. "So what did Duncan mean about the lure of wood slivers?"

"He's referring to the sailboat I built last year."

"A sailboat." She sat back. "Funny, I'd have pictured you with a powerboat. Something large and overbearing."

"Much like myself?"

She laughed then, an easy, rippling sound that reached deep into his soul. "Is this boat the reason you're in such a hurry to get back home?"

"Not the boat, but the trip I'm planning to make in it."

"A trip? Where are you going?"

"Are you always this nosy?"

"I'm a journalist, remember? Now where are you going?"

"Bermuda. The Seychelles. Marshall Islands—"

Her eyes widened. "You're going around the world."

"In time."

"How much time?"

"Three years."

She drew her head back. "Three years in a boat?"

Kyle laughed. "I will be stopping now and then."

"Still, it's an awfully long time." She shifted again, crossing her legs to the other side this time. "Is this trip common knowledge around *Aspects,* and I've just missed it?"

Somehow he couldn't imagine her missing anything. "A few people know—Magda for one."

"She's never mentioned it."

"Magda knows I like to keep my business and personal life separate."

She leaned forward and lowered her voice. "Then why are you telling me?"

He stared into those wide caramel eyes and found he didn't have an answer. "Let's just put it down to moonlight and Vivaldi."

With a soft laugh, she settled back into the corner of the bench again. "What's this sailboat of yours like anyway?"

"A thirty-six-foot yawl."

"Thirty-six feet," she repeated, then rose from the bench and paced it out on the path. "So it is large and overbearing after all," she called as she sauntered back.

Kyle hadn't noticed the breeze until that moment. Hadn't felt it brush his cheek or ruffle his hair. Not until he saw it lift the curls from her shoulders and press the red dress closer against her body, drawing his gaze to the fullness of her breasts, the curve of her waist and the flare of her hips.

This is Jeannie, he reminded himself. Reckless, impudent, not his type at all. Yet even as he resisted the urge to let his gaze skim over her a second time, he couldn't stop the rush of desire she stirred in him.

He could imagine himself moving closer, too close, pinning her against the wall so she couldn't escape. Feeling for himself what the dress only hinted at, and finding out if the rest of her skin was as soft as her hands—knowing instinctively that it would be.

She stopped in front of him. "Is something wrong?"

"No." He rose from the bench. "Just thinking you must be cold."

"I'm okay—"

But he already had his jacket off and was arranging it on her shoulders.

She glanced down. "It's a little big."

"It's perfect," he muttered, pleased with the way it completely engulfed her.

Jeannie shrugged and pulled the lapels of the jacket closer together, surprised at how good the lingering

warmth of Kyle's body felt against her skin. It was odd.
From another man, the old-fashioned gesture may have
seemed contrived. But from Kyle, it seemed perfectly
natural. The same way his concern for her had been natural.

She snuggled deeper into the jacket, feeling the comforting weight on her shoulders as she breathed in the
scent of him; letting it fill her head and indulging, just
for a moment, that side of her that longed to shelter under
the protection of a strong and powerful man like Kyle
Hunter—something she hadn't done for a very long time.

She looked up to find him studying her, his eyes probing and intense. And hungry? No, that was just her over-
active imagination.

Embarrassed, she smiled ruefully at the jacket. "I must
look pretty silly."

"Not at all." The truth was she'd never looked better.
For a brief moment, Kyle knew she'd been somewhere
else. The Boulderbottom boldness and audacity had
slipped away, leaving only Jeannie behind.

And who was she? he wondered. This woman who
could frustrate and confuse him one minute, then touch
him so deeply the next.

He reached out to brush a stray curl from her face.
"So," he said softly, "are you ready to call off the bet?"

Victoria snapped into place. "And see the end of 'Marrying Well'?" She tore off the jacket and threw it at him.
"Forget it."

Head down and moving fast, Jeannie headed back to
the inn.

Kyle fell into step beside her. "I didn't say it for that
reason."

"I don't care what your reason is, Kyle. The outcome
would be the same." She stopped short and turned on
him, her face flushed, fierce. Beautiful. "I've never

backed down from anything in my life. And I'm not about to start now.''

He wanted to reach out, soothe her. Instead, he backed up a step. ''It won't be as easy as you think, Jeannie. Wealthy men are cautious. Always on guard for women who are after their money.''

''I'm not after their money, remember?''

''That's right. You're in this for thirty-three percent of the magazine.''

Her eyes grew round. ''Is that what you think?''

''What other reason is there?''

Her voice softened as she came toward him. ''Love, Kyle. I wouldn't marry for any other reason.''

''I don't believe you.''

She gave a small, self-mocking laugh. ''I'm not surprised. Not with this bet between us. But I'm no different from every other woman. I want the same things they do.'' Her touch was tentative, her fingertips a mere whisper against his chest. ''A little love, tenderness. And that one special man who'll make all the difference.'' She lifted her face to him, her lips trembling, trying to smile. ''Is that so hard to believe?''

He went to wrap his arms around her, but she whirled away, leaving him grasping at nothing.

''Obviously not.'' She grinned and started along the path again. ''Who knows? Maybe this won't be so difficult after all.''

Now we're even, she thought and actually managed to put a few steps between them before his hand closed on her arm, spinning her around to face him.

''You may just be right,'' he muttered, pulling her in.

His gaze shifted, locking on her mouth, the hunger undeniable this time. She saw it in the brightness of his eyes, felt it in the urgency of his touch as his hands moved over her back, pressing her closer.

Okay, she thought. She could handle this. Maybe it was even what she wanted. One kiss to end the curiosity.

Distance. The warning echoed somewhere inside her head as she curled her fingers into his hair. She should pull away. And she would. Very soon. But it was just so good to be close for now. To mold herself to him as he moved her back against the wall, knowing what was to come and bending to it. If only for a moment.

But a moment obviously wasn't what he had in mind. Not when he cupped her face in his hands, his thumbs leisurely tracing the line of her jaw, the curve of her cheek, the fullest part of her lips. And she realized she wasn't ready after all.

Passion this dark was always hot and all consuming, demanding everything and giving nothing. That she was ready for. That she could handle and ultimately reject. But not this. Not this slow, sweet enchantment that was his kiss.

He touched his lips to hers, his tongue taunting and teasing; coaxing her mouth to open, only to leave her waiting, breathless, while he tilted her head back farther, angling her as he wanted and building her need higher and higher.

He was leading her to a place where she didn't know the rules, where her footing was uncertain. A place where she was no longer in control.

She thought of pulling away, but he tightened his grip and she clung to him, feeling the pounding of his heart against her breasts. Her own heart picked up the beat and his pulse echoed through her body, swelling and building as it settled between her thighs, threatening to turn her to liquid.

She moaned softly when at last his mouth was on hers, his tongue probing deeply, exactly as she wanted it. Exactly as he had made her want it.

Jeannie knew she could lose herself in this. Lose everything she was, everything she wanted to be, and just let herself drown in the feel of his mouth, the strength of his touch and the glorious, swirling ache deep inside. And she wouldn't care until it was too late.

His body suddenly tensed and he straightened, setting her abruptly on her feet, holding on just long enough for her to gain her balance.

Dazed and confused, Jeannie could only watch as he bent to pick up his jacket.

"You might be right about this being easy," he said. "But just to be sure, you better take this." He pulled a disk from his pocket, lifted her hand and slapped it into her palm. His dimples deepened as he smiled. "I have a feeling you're going to need it."

5

Jeannie closed one eye, lined up the metal drum at the far end of the garage and took the shot. The empty tin left her hand and soared up, skimming the ceiling lights as it tumbled end over end above the Corvette's gleaming black roof. Above the rear window, it began its descent, falling slowly toward the drum. Jeannie stretched up on her toes and held her breath. The shot was going wide.

"Come on," she muttered, clenching her fists and leaning to the right, as though willpower alone could change its course. The tin hit the rim of the drum, hovered a moment, then pitched forward, clattering to the bottom where it joined the other three.

She smacked the hood of the car. "Four for four. Not bad for the first oil change of the season." She smiled over her shoulder. "And you owe me five bucks."

Magda stood in the door of the garage, scowling as she rummaged through her shoulder bag. "Why do I always fall for this?" She fished out a five and waved it in the air. "Want to go for double or nothing on the spark plugs?"

Jeannie snapped the bill from her friend's fingers. "Not on your life."

"That's because you know you can't do it," Magda grumbled.

"Exactly." Jeannie shoved the bill into the pocket of

her coveralls and grabbed a cloth to wipe her hands. "So how come you can't stay?"

"Because I have a date. I met a most charming director on Saturday, and he called the office this morning. We're having a picnic supper in Galena and, with any luck, I won't be back for days. But I wanted to show you something before I go." She glanced at her watch. "And I just have time for a cup of coffee while I do. Will you be much longer?"

Jeannie tossed the rag into the box. "Not at all. In fact, it's time for the moment of truth." She smiled slowly. "Want to go for double or nothing on the start up?"

"I'd rather put the coffee on."

"Chicken."

Magda flapped her arms then tossed her scarf over her shoulder and trotted out to the street where her candy-apple red convertible blocked the driveway. Curious, Jeannie watched her lean over the back seat, drag out a cooler and lug it back up to the house. "If you'd spent all night making this stuff, you wouldn't leave it out here, either," she said as she passed Jeannie, then scowled and continued on. "Just hurry up."

Jeannie laughed and took hold of the support bar, stepping back as she released the hood. After more than thirty years, it still closed cleanly, with authority—a testament to the loving care the car had been given.

Sliding into the driver's seat, she closed the door and inserted the key. Barely breathing, she pressed the gas down and turned the ignition. The engine fired without hesitation and ran with a steady, even beat. Jeannie smiled as she let out the clutch and backed out of the garage. Tia would be pleased.

Parking at the end of the narrow driveway, Jeannie climbed out and let the engine idle, feeling the same surge of pride she did every spring. She could quote the car's statistics with the best of them: 1963 Stingray

Coupe, split window, four speed, Al-Fin brake drums—
the list went on and on. But none of that mattered to
Jeannie. The important thing was that she had been en-
trusted with its care.

The Corvette had been her aunt's treasure, her indul-
gence, her child. But above all, the car was Tia's leg-
acy—the last laugh on a world that had tried to tell her
she couldn't have all the things she wanted, including a
black muscle car. And the idea of losing that car to Kyle
Hunter was unthinkable.

Even now, days later, Jeannie could still feel the sting
of humiliation every time she thought about the way
she'd melted against him, her reason slowly slipping
away on a single mind-numbing kiss. Yet none of it made
sense.

Kyle was strong and dynamic, accustomed to winning
and having his orders followed without question—exactly the kind of man Jeannie had spent years avoiding.
But when he kissed her, all the convictions and truths she
knew about herself and what she wanted from life van-
ished. And in their place? A desire so stark and simple,
it left her weak, wanting nothing more than to lose herself
in the very strength that repelled her. And if there was
anything she hated, it was a weak woman.

"Coffee's ready," Magda hollered from the porch.

"On my way." Pushing Kyle from her mind, Jeannie
shut off the engine and sprinted across the lawn.

"Why don't we sit out here?" Magda suggested as
Jeannie climbed the stairs. "You know how I love the
outdoors."

"I know how you hate my kitchen."

"There's that, too," Magda conceded. "I've never
seen a house with such a small kitchen."

"Ah, but it has a great garage," Jeannie pointed out
as she led the way along the hall to the kitchen. "What

did you bring me?'' she asked as she stepped into the bathroom to wash her hands.

''A couple of things,'' Magda called over the rushing water. '''Marrying Well' hit the stands this morning, and I figured you wouldn't have seen it yet, so I picked up a few copies.''

Jeannie carried a towel into the kitchen and smiled at the stack of magazines Magda had laid on the table. ''A few?''

''So who counts?'' Magda took a mug from the cupboard. ''You want coffee?''

''Please.'' Jeannie flipped the towel over the back of a chair as she sat down. Pulling a magazine from the pile, she turned to the Boulderbottom column and quickly scanned the page. Everything was just as she'd written it. Kyle hadn't changed a thing, which pleased her more than it should have. The piece was good. She didn't need his approval to know that. She looked up at Magda. ''Any reader reactions?''

''Let's just say the phones were still ringing when I left and the fax machine couldn't keep up. Some hated the idea, of course, but the majority loved it.'' Magda set a cup in front of Jeannie then opened the fridge. ''Any cream in here?''

''On the door.'' Jeannie closed the magazine and tapped her fingers on the cover. ''And Kyle?'' she asked, annoyed that it should matter. ''What did he think?''

''I don't know. He didn't say anything about it.''

''Figures.'' He just couldn't admit she was right.

''But he did ask where you were,'' Magda said as she sat down. ''I told him it was Start-Up Day and he seemed to know what I meant.''

''At least he has a good memory.'' Jeannie splashed cream into her coffee then stood up, suddenly restless. ''Let's take these outside, after all.''

As they passed the dining room, Magda paused and

gestured at the computer screen sitting on the table. "Is that your next Boulderbottom column?"

"I wish." Jeannie wandered into her makeshift office and slumped into a chair. "It's Kyle's proposal for a Boulderbottom series. He handed it to me at the gala, if you can believe it."

"I can." Magda leaned over the screen. "How is it?"

"Don't even ask."

"That bad, huh?"

"Worse. I hate everything about it. The name, the locations, the agenda. But most of all, I hate the fact that I didn't think of it. The idea is perfect for Victoria." Jeannie sighed and sipped at her coffee. "And I promised myself I wouldn't even look at it."

Magda hoisted herself up onto the corner of the table. "Then why did you?"

Jeannie rocked the chair back and stared at the ceiling. "Because it was like this living thing in my purse all weekend. Every time I opened it, there it was, this one silver eye staring up at me. I even tried burying the damn thing in a drawer, but I swear it called to me all night long. When I got up this morning, I couldn't stand it anymore."

Magda settled back a little farther. "So tell me this idea of his that's so wonderful."

"It's called 'Outside Love.'" Jeannie twisted the monitor around. "Read for yourself."

While Magda read, Jeannie set her cup down, closed her eyes and leaned back. She didn't need to look at Kyle's proposal again. She knew it by heart.

Drawing on the popularity of sports and adventure vacations among men, 'Outside Love' had Victoria Boulderbottom, a confessed hedonist and layabout, investigating the question that burned in the mind of every soft-bottomed woman in America: Is it possible for the soft and complacent to find true love among the fit and the frantic?

The series started with a cycling trip in the Grand Canyon, ended with a llama trek in Idaho, and by the end of the first page, Jeannie had known exactly what tone the series would take.

Clad in brightly colored bicycle shorts and a fetching helmet, Victoria would be lounging in the van that followed the cyclists, sipping a chilled power beverage and saving herself for the evening's festivities.

Jeannie would be the one in practical shoes and a sweaty T-shirt, pedaling frantically just to keep up, but that had nothing to do with it. She was only the legwork. Victoria was the delivery, and the column would always reflect her slightly skewed view of life and men. A point which Kyle obviously understood.

Magda swiveled the monitor around. "He's got Victoria pegged—no doubt about that. Not that I'm surprised. He's always had the most amazing ability to tune in to people and trends. It's why he's been successful."

"Don't I know it." Jeannie plunked her chin on her fists and stared at the screen. "If he'd only discussed the idea with me, even once, I'd be touring the Grand Canyon right now instead of sitting here worrying about my aunt Tia's Corvette."

"You're not going to lose it," Magda assured her.

"I'm not so sure anymore," Jeannie admitted, surprising herself as much as Magda. "Meeting Duncan Fox proved once and for all that I could never marry anyone just for money. Or to win a bet, for that matter. And to be honest, I'm not so sure Victoria could, either." Sitting up, she dragged her cup toward her. "Maybe Kyle was right after all. Maybe the whole idea is ridiculous."

"All those telephone calls and faxes say it's not," Magda told her firmly. "You've touched a chord with people, Jeannie. Sparked their curiosity. And I'm sure if Kyle was honest, he'd agree with me."

Jeannie stared into her coffee. "You know him well, don't you?"

"As well as anyone."

Jeannie swirled her cup, watching the coffee rise dangerously close to the edge, but falling just in time, staying inside where it belonged. Nice and safe. "He was at the gala with LeeAnne Alexander last night. Do they see a lot of each other?"

"My sources tell me they've been spotted together quite a bit lately, which doesn't surprise me. She's his type."

Jeannie swirled the cup again. The coffee reached higher this time, touching the lip, receding. "And what type is that?"

"Refined, elegant and truly boring."

"Do you think it's serious?"

She tilted her head to the side. "Why so many questions about Kyle's love life all of a sudden?" Magda's eyes widened. "You're thinking of lining him up as the rich husband, aren't you?"

Jeannie kept her gaze fixed on the coffee, watching it rise and fall. "Not even close."

"But he'd be such an interesting choice. All that raw masculinity wrapped up and set at the feet of Victoria Boulderbottom." Magda sat back, nodding. "I could like that."

Jeannie slapped the cup down, spilling coffee on the table, the margin of safety passed. "Forget it. He's not on the dance card. Besides, he's my boss."

Magda laughed. "When has that ever stopped you? You and Marcus were quite an item for a while as I recall."

"We were buddies. He'd come over with a bottle of wine and we'd talk about what we want to be when we grow up. That's why he went to Alaska. I got so tired of hearing about this dream he had of getting back to the land, that I told him to do it or shut up. So he did." She winced and looked up at Magda. "But don't you dare tell Kyle. He'd hold it against me forever."

"He's not that bad."

Jeannie hit the exit key and shut down the computer. "Maybe not, but he's still not on the dance card."

"Too bad." Magda slid off the table and picked up her purse. "I almost forgot. I still have your messages." Reaching into her bag, she pulled out a bundle of yellow slips and dropped them in front of Jeannie. "Nothing exciting. Except a call from Elliot Daniels."

Jeannie perked up. "Elliot Daniels?" Grabbing the bundle, she snapped off the elastic band. "Are you sure?"

"Are you Catholic?"

"Sorry." Jeannie spread the slips on the table. "Here it is. 'Elliot Daniels, 9:15.'" She pushed back the chair and stood up. "This is great."

Magda looked skeptical. "You know who Elliot Daniels is don't you?"

"Not really. I ran into him at the gala while I was waiting for the valet to bring my car around." She started to pace. "I'm surprised he even remembered me."

"Well, do yourself a favor and forget about him."

Jeannie kept moving. "Why?"

"Because he's Kyle's best friend."

Jeannie stopped and looked at her. "Now that you mention it, I do remember seeing him with Kyle at the bar." She waved a hand. "We'll double-date."

"Do you really think Kyle's going to let you get involved with Elliot?"

Jeannie studied the slip of yellow paper. Maybe not, she admitted to herself. But this whole thing was Kyle's fault. And Elliot was just too good to pass up.

"Kyle doesn't have to know," she said at last. "The very fact that Elliot called means he hasn't said anything to Kyle yet. And we both know Kyle's going to New York tomorrow for three days." She tacked Elliot's number to the board above her phone. "A lot can happen in three days, Magda. An awful lot." And when she took thirty-three percent of the magazine, she wasn't going to feel bad at all.

Magda shrugged her purse strap over her shoulder and headed for the front door. "I wish I could stay and talk you out of this, but I have to run."

"I'll let you know how it goes," Jeannie said when they reached the car.

Magda tossed her purse into the back seat. "You better. I'll be at the Four Cousins Bed and Breakfast...." She stopped, one hand on the door, the other raised, shielding her eyes as she focused on something down the street. "Well, well. What have we here?"

Jeannie followed her gaze. A silver Jag had just turned the corner and was heading toward them.

Magda lowered her hand. "Isn't this interesting."

"What?"

The Jag pulled in across the road and parked, but Jeannie couldn't see the driver through the tinted glass. "Who is it?"

"Kyle."

Jeannie froze, feeling her stomach slide. "What's he doing here?"

Magda smiled at her. "Editorial meeting?"

Kyle stepped out onto the sidewalk, squinting for a moment as his eyes adjusted to the bright sunlight. Jeannie knew she was staring, but couldn't seem to look away.

If he had looked good in a tuxedo, he looked even better now in light trousers and a sweater the color of summer wheat—the same color as his hair in the sunshine, she realized. A rare shade of pure gold shot with white.

He looked directly at her and she felt herself straighten, unconsciously moving her shoulders back the extra bit that would make her breasts more pronounced—a subtle and timeless invitation.

He stayed by his car for the longest time, just watching her. Yet there was nothing about him that suggested he was waiting to be asked. He would come when he was ready, of that she had no doubt.

Magda lowered her voice. "Sure you don't want to change your mind about that dance card?"

Jeannie gave her head a quick shake and glanced down at her shoes. "Positive." She cleared her throat and tried again. "Positive."

She tried to concentrate on her shoes, the car, anything to avoid meeting his gaze. But he was too compelling. She lifted her eyes and he came toward her, his steps slow and measured.

She felt sloppy and dirty all of a sudden in her greasy coveralls, but resisted the urge to check the side mirror of Magda's convertible. She wouldn't give him the satisfaction.

He stopped in front of her and Jeannie raised an eyebrow in question, not trusting her voice.

"I remembered it was Start-Up Day," he explained. "And I figured I'd come by and see the car." He paused. "I hope you don't mind."

She should have known. "You're welcome to look, but I assure you, you're wasting your time."

His eyes held hers a moment longer. "Possibly," he murmured, then shifted his attention to Magda. "I'll understand if you were leaving."

"It's always good to see you, Kyle," she said lightly, then turned to Jeannie, her eyes narrow and cunning. "Call me."

As Magda pulled away, Jeannie squared her shoulders for the standoff. "I'm awfully busy, but since you're here, you might as well take a look at the car." She gave him a thin smile. "It'll do you good to see exactly what you're missing."

He smiled. "Do you know you have grease on your nose?"

Jeannie shoulders sagged. "I've been working," she muttered, running the heel of her hand over her nose.

"You're making it worse. Come here." Cupping her face in his hands, Kyle gently rubbed his thumbs across the bridge of her nose.

Jeannie gritted her teeth, but couldn't quite bring herself to pull away. "I can do this myself."

"Just hold still," he scolded when she screwed up her face. "What have you been doing anyway?"

"Changing the oil."

"By yourself?"

"Why not?"

"No reason." He backed up a step. "There. Perfect again."

For him, maybe. "I'm not going to thank you."

"I didn't think you would."

He was doing it again, Jeannie thought and crossed to where the Corvette sat waiting. "Do you want me to open the hood?"

"To be honest, the car's not the only reason I'm here."

"Let me guess. You heard about the reaction to 'Marrying Well' and came by to find out what color I've selected for my new office."

He laughed. "Not exactly."

"Then you couldn't wait a moment longer to find out what I thought about your series. Is that it?"

"I'm curious, yes."

Jeannie braced a hip against the door. "Okay. It's good. Absolutely perfect for Victoria. Happy?"

"I should be. But I'm not." He leaned back against the car and lifted his face to the sun. "Because now it will never see the light of day, no matter how good it is, unless I change the format completely."

Jeannie stared at him. "Why not?"

"Because whether you win or lose, Victoria will be finished once 'Marrying Well' is over." He opened one eye and looked at her. "You have thought of that, haven't you?"

"Yes," she admitted, her anger quickly losing its edge.

"Does it bother you?"

Jeannie shrugged as she strolled the length of her car. "A little. I always knew Victoria wouldn't last forever, and this is the best way for her to go out, on a blaze of glory instead of with a whimper." She paused and looked back at him, surprised by what she was going to say next. "And to be honest, I'm ready for a change."

"I'm not surprised."

"Why?"

"Because Victoria has a limited range. I can understand why you'd feel restricted after a while."

Jeannie gave her head a shake. "That's the strange thing. I wasn't feeling restricted at all. I enjoyed the anonymity of being the notorious Lady Victoria Boulderbottom. But now that I know it's going to be over, I'm looking forward to writing about other things."

Kyle followed as she wandered back to the porch. "Like what?"

"Health care, the environment, all the things that used to bore Victoria to tears. And me, too, for a while I must admit." She gave her head a shake. "I guess it all sounds pretty trite to you."

"Jeannie, there's nothing trite about any of those issues." Kyle sat down on the step next to her. "Why would your interest in them be?"

Avoiding his gaze, she leaned down and plucked a blade of grass. "Because it's straight out of journalism school, isn't it? Change the world, one small voice and all that. Earnest sentiments and well-meant, but overdone."

"Then find a way new way to say it," Kyle said softly.

Jeannie twirled the grass between her fingers, feeling the strength of a rarely voiced dream beginning to build. "That's exactly what I want to do. There has to be some way to make it all matter to the guy sitting in the Laundromat who just got laid off. Or the woman on the subway who had to leave a sick baby with the sitter because she couldn't afford to miss a day's pay."

She tossed the blade of grass aside and stood up, turning her back on Kyle to walk the width of the lawn. "I want to use everything I learned as Victoria Boulderbottom to make the issues real. To make them matter."

She glanced back at him, suddenly embarrassed by the passion of her own speech. "But you see, I'm already deadly dull just talking about it."

Kyle shook his head. "You may be many things, Jeannie, but dull will never be one of them." He got to his feet and crossed to where she stood. "And I believe you'll do it. You'll find a way." He paused, his eyes searching hers. "But I don't think that's all you want."

Jeannie looked away, wondering how he knew. "You're right. I want recognition this time. I want my name on the byline. I want a Pulitzer. Maybe even a spot on 'Oprah.'" She made a frame with her hands. "'America's News Goddesses—What Are They Really Like?'" She let her arms drop. "I guess I'm pretty transparent."

"Not at all."

"Then how did you know?"

"I told you before. We think alike. Which brings me back to the reason I came. I have something for you."

"Another assignment?"

"No. A present." He turned and started down the driveway. "Come on. It's in my car."

Jeannie stared after him. Did he practice, or was it a gift, she wondered, this ability to throw her off balance from one moment to the next? She jogged a few steps to catch up to him. "What kind of present?"

"The kind you open."

"But why?"

"Because after I bought it, I couldn't think of anyone else to give it to." He took a package from the front seat and handed it to her.

She held the parcel at arm's length, eyeing it warily. "Will it explode when I open it?"

"Of course not. It's programmed to go off after I leave."

She lifted only her eyes to him. "I should have known."

His dimples deepened as his smile broadened. "Just open it."

It was strange, but as much as Jeannie found his dimples out of place in a face that was all hard lines and angles, she couldn't imagine that smile without them anymore.

Dangerous notions, she reminded herself and concentrated on the package, testing the edges with her thumbs. There was a lot of padding in there, so it had to be something fragile. Yet it was hard and light at the same time.

She tapped her fingers on the bottom. Whatever it was, she couldn't accept it. Not after last night. But she could open it. Take a quick look and then hand it back. What harm could that do?

Kyle couldn't hold back a grin as Jeannie shoved her sleeves up past her elbows and tore into the wrapping. There was no thoughtful search for the tape. No careful folding of paper. Only impatient fingers and muttered curses as she went at the package in the same way she went at everything—full speed and aiming straight for the heart.

It was the reason her work at *Aspects* was so good. And the reason her kiss still burned on his lips.

Looking up, she demanded to know, "Who wrapped this, anyway?" then bent to tackle the corrugated cardboard liner—the last obstacle between Jeannie and her goal.

It was amazing, but even in a pair of baggy coveralls and smelling faintly of lemons and motor oil, there was something undeniably appealing about Jeannie Renamo.

It would take years to even begin to know every facet of her, or understand what went on inside her head. She could be a fascinating journey or a trip into hell, depending on a man's point of view. But one thing she would never be was easy. And easy was what he needed most right now.

The cardboard sprang back, revealing the back of a heavy wooden frame and a hand-written card. "You were right. Victoria belongs to you."

Jeannie sent him a quick, questioning glance then wiped her palms on her coveralls and flipped the picture over. A half smile curved her lips. "So, it was you."

Drawn as much by the unexpected softness in her voice as the question itself, Kyle moved closer. "What was me?"

"The one who beat me to this picture."

She gazed at the photograph as though not quite believing what she held in her hands. As though he had set some great treasure before her, when in truth it was only a shot of an unknown woman and a soldier, taken by someone who had never achieved any measure of fame—worthless in terms of real money except for the frame. "I don't understand," Kyle admitted.

The gilt edging shimmered in the sunlight as she tipped the frame up. "When I saw this at the gala, there was something about the woman that made me want to buy it. It was as though I could hear her laughing. At him, at me, at the world. After Ellie told me the story, I knew I had to have it. But someone had been there before me." She lifted her face to him, her eyes wide with wonder. "You."

Her lips were only inches from his now, moist and full, parted in a tender smile, and it seemed to Kyle that there was only one response possible.

Kissing her now would be completely different from last time. Deeper, more sensual, the kind of kiss a woman gives to a man when he has touched her heart. It wouldn't take much. Just a matter of leaning closer, brushing his lips against hers and tasting her slowly, thoroughly.

He unconsciously reached to cup her chin in his hand, only catching himself when she turned back to the photograph.

"Did Ellie tell you the story?"

"What? Yes. Something about him calling off the wedding," he answered, annoyed that the details had escaped him at the moment.

Jeannie tilted her head to one side, her attention still on the picture. "I think she was well rid of him, but I wish I knew what happened to her afterward."

Kyle looked down at the photograph. He hadn't thought much about it. All he had seen was Victoria Boulderbottom, triumphant even in the face of defeat. But now Jeannie had sparked his curiosity. "What do you think happened?"

Jeannie's expression turned wistful. "She lived a long and happy life, doing the things she always dreamed about."

"Winning Pulitzers perhaps?"

Her smile was decidedly cheeky. "Perhaps."

"Well, she's yours now, and you can decide whatever fate you want for her."

A shadow passed over Jeannie's face as she ran a hand over the frame. Then she laid the photograph on the wrapping and turned her back. "Thanks, Kyle, but it's out of the question."

6

Kyle grabbed her arm, making her face him. "Why?"

His grip wasn't meant to hold her. She could have shaken him off easily, but she didn't. Instead, she stood her ground, meeting his gaze with one that was equally determined. "Because I hate being in anyone's debt."

"For God's sake, it's a picture, not a diamond."

"But there's still an implied obligation if I take it."

"What obligation?"

"Why don't you tell me?"

He nodded slowly. "This is about the other night, isn't it?"

"Not at all." Her gaze slipped away as she broke free. "I simply don't accept gifts from a man unless I'm serious about him. As for the other…" She shrugged and started across the road. "It was a kiss. No big deal. Let's just put it down to…what was it you said? Moonlight and Vivaldi."

Kyle tucked the picture under his arm and followed. "If you like."

"What would you call it then?" Jeannie called over her shoulder. "Curiosity, maybe? Lust, perhaps? Okay, I'll go for those. I'll even take some of the blame." Inside the garage, she stopped and crouched beside the rag box. "But as pleasant as it was, it's a nonissue now."

"Pleasant? Is that what you'd call it?"

His sexy smile was infuriating, so she focused on the cloths instead. "Okay, very pleasant. But it's finished."

"Then why won't you look at me?"

If the smile was bad, his candor was worse. She straightened and faced him. "I'm looking at you now. Satisfied?"

"No." Slowly he closed the distance between them. "I haven't figured out what happened between us, either, Jeannie. But I know I spent the weekend thinking about it, and you. And I'll admit right now, that I'd like nothing more than to pick up where we left off. But I can't, and I know that, too. Not as long as this bet exists."

Taking her hand, he stroked his thumb across her palm. Too quickly, the warmth spread farther than her fingertips, curling slowly through her like smoke from a fire that just wouldn't die.

"I was wrong to kiss you, Jeannie. And I give you my word, it will never happen again."

She pulled away, holding back the protest that came unexpectedly to her lips. This was perfect, exactly what she wanted. Whatever power he had over her was too strong, too quick. No man should be able to make a woman feel everything so intensely. The rage, the tenderness but most of all the wanting was much too much to be right. Or safe.

It was better this way. And the gnawing inside only meant that she was hungry.

Turning away, she grabbed a bucket from the shelf. "Well, it's nice to know we're on the same wavelength. It'll make things easier once we're partners. Now, if you'll excuse me, I have a car to wash." She nodded at the picture as she pushed past him. "You should wrap that up. It'll get filthy in here."

"Then take it into the house."

"I can't."

"Because it's a present?"

"Yes."

"Then think of it as a presentation instead." He held up the picture. "Jeannie Renamo," he said, his voice deep and theatrical, "the management and staff of *Aspects* magazine take great pleasure in presenting you with this token of our appreciation for a job well-done." He dropped the lofty tones. "No strings attached. What do you say?"

Jeannie closed her eyes. How could a man be so exasperating and so endearing at the same time? "No" was the answer she wanted to give. "No" would solve everything. But it seemed so petty all of a sudden. Especially now that they understood each other.

The bucket clattered to the ground. "Okay, I'll take it. But only because I love her." Pressing the frame close to her chest, Jeannie dashed across the driveway to the front porch.

She took the stairs two at a time and didn't look back until she reached the front door. "Thanks again, Kyle. I'll see you at the office."

In the living room, Jeannie knelt beside the coffee table and balanced the picture against a heavy candle, wondering how two people who never saw anything eye-to-eye could ever have been attracted to the same face.

The answer was Victoria, of course—the only thing she and Kyle had in common other than the bet. And one kiss. One hot, wonderful kiss that had kept him awake, too, she recalled with just a touch of smugness. But he had given his word it would never happen again. And she believed him.

"Well, I can handle it if you can, Kyle Hunter." She pushed herself to her feet. "Probably better."

As she walked to the door, Elliot's message by the phone caught her eye. Lifting the receiver, Jeannie punched in the numbers. On the fourth ring, an answering machine clicked in, promising Elliot would call if she left a message. When she was finished speaking, she winked at Victoria and hung up again. They were back on track again, thanks to Kyle's visit.

Feeling a sudden generosity of spirit toward him, she also decided that Magda was right—Kyle wasn't such a bad guy after all. And she was halfway down the front stairs before she spotted him, sleeves rolled up and hose in hand, spraying water on her Corvette, proving once again how wrong she could be.

She leapt off the third step. "What are you doing?"

Kyle smiled over the roof of the car. "You took so long, I decided to start without you. Have to protect my interests, you understand." He gestured with the hose. "Hand me that bottle of shampoo will you?"

She look down at the spot where he was pointing. Cleaner, wax, cloths—everything was laid out neatly on the grass. "Where did you get these?"

"From the garage." He nodded at the bottles again. "Shampoo, please."

"Listen, Kyle. Nobody touches this car but me. Nobody."

"Never mind. I'll get it myself. Do you have another sponge? I could use a hand."

Jeannie snatched up the shampoo. "Move away from my car."

Kyle walked the length of the Corvette, wetting down the sides and tugging the hose behind him. "Yours now," he taunted. "But who knows how it will all turn out?"

She stalked him around the car. "I'll show you how it will turn out if you don't get away from that car right now."

Kyle dropped the hose and held up his hands. "You win, but it wouldn't be a bad idea to let me help. Not only will the job go faster, but regardless of how this bet turns out, I think we should get to know each other a little better than we do now. On a friendly level.''

She tapped the shampoo bottle against her leg. He had a point. How could she continue to work with him or hope to be his partner if she couldn't even spend an hour with him? "Okay, you can help." She tossed the bottle to him. "But we do it my way. Remember that."

Jeannie took one more swipe at the hood with the buffing cloth. "What do you think?"

Kyle glanced up as he wound the last of the hose around the reel. "Looks great."

Satisfied, Jeannie pitched the cloth aside, then lay back on the lawn, closing her eyes and letting the heat of the sun soothe her tired muscles. "You know what's strange," she said on a sigh. "I've been doing this on my own for so long, that I'd forgotten how nice it can be to have help." She opened her eyes at the sound of his footsteps beside her. "Thanks."

He loomed over her—very tall, very broad and very appealing. "You're welcome."

Jeannie closed her eyes again before she could be accused of staring. The time had passed quite successfully and she didn't need anything to upset the balance now.

The truth was that Kyle had surprised her. He hadn't tried to tell her how to do the work, or offered to go and get another brand of cleaner or wax—his personal favorite, of course—or entertained her with endless stories about himself.

He had simply let her get on with the job, and had done the same himself, giving her Corvette the kind of careful attention she did herself. Whether it was because he respected the importance of the car to her, or because he had a stake in it, she wasn't sure, but she appreciated his effort.

"Are you hungry?" he asked as he stretched out beside her.

"Starving."

"So am I." His arm brushed against her as he folded his hands behind his head. "Want to go get some lunch?"

She wrinkled her nose and tried to ignore the warmth that was pooling deep inside her. A warmth that had nothing to do with the sun and everything to do with the fact that Kyle was lying too close.

Lunch would only complicate things, but after he'd worked so hard, it didn't seem right to send him away hungry.

"I'd have to clean up first," she warned.

"I'm in no hurry."

"Well, then, there's a place about two blocks over. Basically roadhouse, but it's good."

"Sounds great." One blue eye opened and peered at her. "And it'll give me chance to test-drive the Corvette."

Jeannie only laughed. "Dream on. I'm the only one who drives that car."

"We'll see." Kyle got to his feet and extended a hand to her. "Come on."

"We're in luck," Jeannie called as she rummaged through the fridge. "Iced tea and real lemons." Straightening, she juggled ice, fruit and a pitcher to the table, then kicked the fridge door closed with her foot and grinned at Kyle. "All you need to do is grab a couple of glasses from the cupboard and we'll be set."

While Jeannie cut the fruit, Kyle dropped ice into two glasses and poured the tea. "Are you planning a picnic?" he asked as sat down.

Jeannie handed him a slice of lemon. "No. Why?"

"Because there's a cooler beside me." He lifted the lid. "And it's jammed full."

"Magda's picnic supper." Jeannie groaned. "I don't believe we both forgot it." She leaned over the cooler. "There's enough food in here to last a week."

"Why don't we forget the roadhouse?"

Jeannie drummed her fingers on the table. "I guess if Magda wanted the food that bad, she would have come back for it by now. It would be a shame to see everything go to waste."

Kyle leaned back and stretched his legs out next to her. "Then we'll be sure to let her know how it was."

Jeannie moved back a step, thinking Magda was right. The kitchen really was too small. "Okay," she said, and took a long swallow of the iced tea. "But I still have to clean up. I can't eat like this."

"I wouldn't mind washing up myself."

She pointed to the door by the fridge. "Through there. Towels are fresh."

Kyle closed the door behind him and glanced around. Like the rest of Jeannie's house, the bathroom was small, but bright and comfortable. There were none of the fancy soaps and overgrown ferns that always cluttered Lee-Anne's bathroom. Just big, thick towels, a sparkling claw-foot tub and a counter that was clear except for a single glass, a bar of soap and a pump bottle of hand lotion.

He turned on the tap and worked the soap into a lather, releasing the same light citrus fragrance that he had detected on Jeannie that morning. Kyle closed his eyes, letting her scent fill his head as he washed, knowing this was as close as he would ever get to it again.

"Just in time," she said when he joined her in the living room a few minutes later.

She was standing beside the sofa, a hammer in one

hand, a small picture hook in the other. "Could you hold Victoria up over the small table for me?"

Kyle propped the picture against the wall. "Here?"

"A little to the left. Perfect. Now stay put while I get a pencil."

Kyle kept the picture level as she dashed back into the kitchen. Across from him, one wall was devoted to a stereo cabinet and racks of CDs while bookcases dominated the walls on either side of the fireplace. Candles adorned the small tables, but the only pictures were those massed on the mantel—wedding portraits, graduation pictures and the laughing faces of children.

"Is that your family?" he asked when Jeannie returned.

"Every one of them." She gave him a lopsided grin as she marked the spot on the wall. "I'm Italian, remember? Aunts, uncles and cousins coming out my ears. How about you?"

"There was only my dad and me for as long as I can remember."

Jeannie frowned. "I can't imagine growing up without hordes of family around. It must have been lonely."

"I've never thought much about it." Kyle crossed to the fireplace and lifted one of the frames. "Who's this?"

"My brother, Pauli, our musician. His hair's much shorter now."

"Is he any good?"

"Very good. In fact, he's got a shot with a major recording company next week. It could be the break he needs."

"Well, I wish him luck." Kyle set the picture down and walked the length of the fireplace, studying the faces that looked back at him. "Lots of kids in here."

"Naturally." Holding the hook in place, she tapped the nail into place. "Drives them all crazy that I don't have any yet."

"Do you even want any?"

The hammer stilled. "Someday, yes. I'd like a house-ful."

"Then I suppose you and everyone else will be delighted if you win this bet."

"I suppose they will." She picked up Victoria and positioned her on the wall. "What about you? Do you ever think about getting married? Having children?"

"Sometimes, but not for a while yet."

"Because of this trip you're planning."

"Exactly." Deciding to leave it at that, Kyle picked up a shot of a much-younger Jeannie and a woman standing beside the Corvette.

"This has to be the aunt who left you the car."

"Tia?" Jeannie straightened Victoria, then came toward him. "That's her."

Tall and erect, Aunt Tia had a presence that demanded attention. While she hugged Jeannie fiercely with one hand, she laid claim to the Corvette with the other, her eyes looking straight into the camera as though daring anyone to step between them. Kyle grimaced. She'd taught Jeannie well.

He set the photograph down and picked up another—a shot of a young couple with a child. Unlike Tia, this woman wasn't interested in the camera at all. She was too busy watching her husband and daughter, her eyes full of love and pride as he held the toddler above his head, their noses just touching.

The child, a little girl with short red curls, was laughing as she reached for him. There was no trace of fear in her expression, or apprehension at the height at which she was being held. She was completely absorbed in the task of grabbing a fistful of his dark hair—confident that he wasn't going to let her fall, that she could trust him to keep her safe.

The man's eyes were soft, his grin broad even though

the child was bent on attack. Kyle couldn't help smiling. He obviously wasn't the first man to be captivated by Jeannie Renamo.

Jeannie's fingers closed on the edge of the frame. "My parents."

"I figured as much. You look very much like your mother."

"So I've been told," Jeannie said evenly then set the picture on the mantel and headed out again. "I'm going to clean up. Put some music on if you like, and help yourself to some more iced tea. I'll be a while."

Kyle followed her into the kitchen and watched her disappear through another door into a bedroom. "I'll get lunch ready if you like."

She emerged with a stack of clothes. "Plates are in the cupboard. Napkins are somewhere. Good luck." The bathroom door closed firmly behind her.

He opened the cupboard, listening to the squeal of the taps as she turned on the water and realizing he hadn't noticed a shower curtain in the bathtub. So she wasn't a woman who took showers, he mused. She took long, hot baths instead, in water perfumed by fragrant soaps.

As he set the plates on the table, he heard the unmistakable sound of a zipper being pulled, followed by the rustle of fabric as the coveralls fell to the floor.

He heard her step into the tub and glanced at the doorknob.

Had he heard the lock click? He was sure he hadn't. He drew in a long breath. Was it an oversight or an invitation? His body started to hum. For a fleeting moment, he thought of how easy it would be to join her in that tub. And how much he wanted to.

He imagined her leaning back, eyes closed, the water lapping around her breasts. Would she reach out to him? Or cover herself and order him out? He took a single step toward the door.

The water splashed again and the lock snapped into place. He had his answer. And just as well. With a wry smile, he set about finding the napkins. The sooner lunch was over, the better.

As he finished laying out Magda's picnic, the lock clicked again. Warm, scented air filled the kitchen as she came through the door. Her face was flushed, her feet bare and she was still tucking her T-shirt into her jeans. She looked drowsy and tousled and completely relaxed— the way she might look after making love, Kyle thought, experiencing a rush of desire so strong, it was close to pain.

"Smells wonderful," she said as she came toward him. She lifted one of the lids. "What's in here?"

Kyle forced himself to focus, to think of anything but the fact that she'd changed her scent again. Something subtle and musky with a hint of...

"Aioli," she said on a sigh. "I love this stuff. And pâté." She cast a quick glance around the table. "Where's the bread?" Reaching in front of him, she tore off a piece of the crusty loaf and spread it with pâté.

She was gone again, lost in the food and the moment, everything else forgotten—which irritated him for some reason.

Holding one hand under the bread, she raised it to her mouth and took a bite. Her eyes closed and she moaned deep in her throat. "You have to try this," she whispered, lifting her bread to him.

His lips touched her fingertips as he took the morsel into his mouth. But instead of letting her draw back, he captured her hand in his and held on. "Good," he said, though he barely tasted it. "Very good."

She swallowed hard. "Do you want more?"

"Definitely."

Slipping her hand from his, she spread pâté on another bit of bread. Her hand trembled slightly this time when he held it. He stroked his thumb across her wrist, pleased to find that her pulse was racing as fast as his own—to know she was as vulnerable to this thing as he was.

"What's next?" he asked, wrapping his arms around her waist, drawing her close.

"Salad?" she said in high little voice that made him smile.

He sank his fingers deep into her hair and eased her head back, impatient now for the one taste that had been on his mind all day. But he'd given his word.

"Salad," he repeated and gently released her.

She smoothed her hands over her hair and cleared her throat. "And some music. I'll just go—"

"Let me," he interrupted, grateful for the excuse.

Kyle crouched in front of the stereo, hoping to find something distracting in Jeannie's collection of CDs. But as he flipped through them, he noticed an LP tucked away at the back of the cabinet. Intrigued, he reached in and carefully lifted it out.

The cover was done in warm sepia tones, lending an air of mystery to the young woman standing in a beam of moonlight at the base of a set of stairs, a lone figure in tattered skirts and ragged shawl. The room around her was barren and the fire cold, but her smile was warm and her eyes bright as she reached out to the man standing in shadow at the top of the stairs.

The writing was in Italian, but Kyle recognized the scene from Puccini's opera *La Bohème*. He glanced up at the mantel then back at the cover. And if the woman playing the part of Mimi wasn't Jeannie's mother, Kyle would be very much surprised.

He carefully withdrew the album, cued the turntable and set the volume. There was a moment of crackling, and then the strings began, followed by a sweet, clear soprano voice—the voice of Jeannie's mother.

"I didn't realize you were an opera fan."

Jeannie stood in the doorway, her mouth set in a thin line.

"Only when it's done well," Kyle said. "And this is very well-done."

"I'm glad you like it."

"That's your mother singing, isn't it?"

Jeannie hesitated a moment, then took the album from him. "I'm surprised you recognized her." Sinking down onto the sofa, she tucked her legs under her and cradled the album in her lap. "Not many people do. But then again, not many people get to see her album."

"I noticed it wasn't well displayed."

She glanced up. "'Hidden' would describe what it was."

Kyle had the grace to smile. "You're right. I'll turn it off."

"No, leave it," Jeannie said and set the cover aside. "I was just surprised, that's all. You see, I have a rule about playing her music for other people. I don't."

Her mother's voice rose in a passionate and sensual burst then sank to an almost breathless finish, leaving behind a haunting silence.

"Too bad," Kyle murmured. "A voice like that should be shared."

Jeannie's response was no more than a whisper. "I've always thought so, too." As the second number began, she leapt up, switched off the turntable and flicked on the CD. Jazz, pleasant but undemanding, filled the room. She rose and headed for the kitchen. "We should eat."

Kyle rose and caught her hand, pulling her back. "I'd rather hear about your mother."

"What's to tell?" Jeannie asked, then leaned down and picked up the album, holding it at arm's length. "She could sing. Mozart, Puccini—you name it."

"And?" Kyle asked gently.

"And she married my father, they moved to the States and she never sang on a stage again. End of story."

"But she was so talented. I can't believe she couldn't make it here."

"That's something we'll never know. Once she stepped off the jet, she was Mrs. Antonio Renamo, nothing more. They ran a business, raised a family and now they play golf in Florida. Everything my father always wanted." Jeannie tossed the album onto the coffee table. "All of her dreams got lost somewhere along the way. And I don't think he ever gave it a second thought."

"Maybe that's what she wanted," Kyle said softly.

"What are you talking about?" Jeannie snapped. "She had an album, Kyle. She tasted success, held it in her hands. And she let my father take it all away."

"He couldn't take what she didn't want to give."

"What are you trying to say?"

"Only that she probably wasn't like you, Jeannie. Maybe she was content with just a taste."

"Come on, Kyle, you don't even know her."

"That's true. But I know you." He took hold of her hands, holding her still. "And I know that no one could take your dreams away. You wouldn't let them."

She lifted her face. "I think that's the first time you've ever been right about anything."

She tried to smile, but her eyes were so tormented that for a moment, Kyle couldn't move. Then he pulled her close, wrapping his arms around her, trying to give her a comfort he sensed had been missing for a very long time.

All the fight slowly drained away and she melted against him, her head fitting securely beneath his chin, her fingers curving on his chest. Leaning back against the wall, Kyle gathered her closer, his strong hands stroking her hair.

Embarrassed now, she tried to pull away, but he

wouldn't have it. Holding her chin with one hand, he touched his lips to hers—moist, soft kisses that asked nothing but that she be comforted. And when that wasn't enough, she reached up, closing her eyes as she curled her fingers into his hair.

He shivered at the first tentative stroke of her tongue and she felt the tension in the taut muscle of his shoulders, the tightening of his fingers as he ran a hand down her back.

He moved one hand into the thick of her hair, holding her firmly while he deepened the kiss. When he lifted her hips, she moved with him, finding the rhythm easy and right.

Slowly, inevitably, he was taking her under again, and she held on harder, wanting nothing more than to carry him with her. But she forced her eyes to open, refusing to believe that his simplest touch could make her forget so quickly. "Kyle, stop."

"Soon," he murmured, his lips finding the spot where her pulse already beat in time to his.

"No," she said. "I want you to stop now."

He drew his head back but didn't step away. She waited, barely breathing and suddenly afraid. Not of him, but of herself and the choice she would make if he bent to her again.

She watched the play of emotion across his face: frustration, confusion and then something she hadn't expected—tenderness. A tenderness that opened her heart just enough to allow him to step inside before the door closed firmly behind him.

Then suddenly he was moving back, giving her what she wanted. And taking away what she needed.

7

The maître d' stood like a sentinel at his post, gold pen at the ready. "Good evening, good evening," he sang as Jeannie and Elliot approached. "And welcome to La Scala. Do you have reservations?"

"A few," Elliot said gravely. "But we came anyway. Daniels, eight o'clock."

Jeannie suppressed a grin as the maître d' grudgingly scratched the name from his list. "Another comedian." He sniffed and plucked two menus from the rack. "Just what this city needs. Follow me, please."

"Takes his job seriously, doesn't he?" Elliot said as he flipped open his menu after being seated.

"And himself," Jeannie agreed. "But I have it on very good authority that the food is worth it."

Elliot glanced up at her. "Being here with you is worth it."

Jeannie smiled, sensing it wasn't just false flattery or a line. Over the past few days, she and Elliot had spoken enough times on the phone for her to determine that he was exactly what she'd judged him to be at the gala—an easygoing, intelligent man with a dry, subtle wit she found enormously attractive.

Her heart didn't race when he stood beside her and her skin was in no danger of becoming overheated at his slightest touch. But he did make her feel relaxed and comfortable. And there was a lot to be said for that.

With Kyle in New York for three days, she'd managed to regain her perspective. Write another column. Start sleeping again. Having the wrong man lodged in her heart wasn't really a problem. She just had to find the right one to replace him, and fast.

"Good evening," a waiter said as he lit the candles. "Would you care to see the wine list?"

While Elliot chose the wine, Jeannie inspected the bread basket the waiter had set in front of her, gently folding back the linen napkin to reveal a row of plump bread sticks, still hot and fragrant with garlic.

"Smells wonderful." She held the basket out to Elliot. "Would you like one?"

"No thanks."

"I admire your restraint. Probably because I have none of my own."

The tiny lines at the corners of his eyes deepened as he smiled. "It's just habit, believe me. So many years of living with a nutritionist I suppose."

Jeannie sat back. There it was again. That same look that came over his face every time his soon-to-be ex-wife crept into the conversation. Nothing bitter or angry like so many separated men she'd met, just completely lost. Which was too bad, because if anyone deserved to be found, it was Elliot Daniels.

The waiter returned with the wine and filled both their glasses. When they were alone again, Elliot reached into the bread basket. "It's about time I started breaking those old habits, don't you think?" He picked up a bread stick, then raised his glass. "To new habits."

Jeannie clicked her glass against his. Elliot Daniels could work, she was certain of it. But there was still the matter of the wife.

Jeannie drummed her fingertips on the stem of her

glass while Elliot devoured the bread stick. Exactly how deep did the hurt go? she wondered. And how long would it take to get him over it? That was the tricky part—time. She simply didn't have any to waste.

Deciding the quickest route was always the most direct one, Jeannie set her glass down, propped her elbows on the table and rested her chin in her hands.

"So tell me, Elliot," she said brightly. "When do you get your divorce?"

Kyle dropped his briefcase beside the hall closet and tossed his jacket on a chair. Three days, fifteen interviews and one pounding headache later he still hadn't come up with a likely candidate for Marcus's job.

If it kept on like this, he wouldn't get out of Chicago until Christmas, a thought that only made his head throb harder.

Swinging around the corner into the kitchen, he yanked open the fridge. One beer left—there was a God. Food would be a good idea, as well, but Kyle decided to unwind for a few minutes first.

He dropped into the soft leather sofa in the living room and switched on the television, surfing the channels for something mindless and easy. He'd done enough thinking in the past three days—the boat, the trip, the interviews. And out of nowhere, always Jeannie.

Not gentle or soothing, something a man could use at the end of a long day. But a storm that churned inside him—dangerous, compelling and impossible to control.

Why now? he wondered. The one time when he didn't need any more complications. And why her?

Too tired to go over it again, Kyle hit the mute button and stood up, noticing the flashing light on his answering machine. "What now?" he grumbled and punched Play.

"Hi, Kyle…"

LeeAnne's voice, smooth as honey.

"You haven't called in a long time."

He could almost see her, eyelashes lowered, lips moist and pouting, ready to forgive him. He sat down on the arm of the sofa. Why couldn't she be the one on his mind?

"I'll be home all day. Call me."

Kyle sighed. There was no point. He drained the last of his beer while the messages rolled on.

"Kyle, Matt here. Bad news. Brian can't crew with us after all, but my cousin Jack could replace him. Let me know if you're interested."

Kyle ran a hand over his face. What choice did he have? A crew of three could never win the race. The next message began.

"Kyle?"

He perked up at the sound of Elliot's voice.

"I wanted you to be the first to know. I took your advice."

This was new. Elliot rarely took anyone's advice. Especially his.

"I have a date tonight."

Kyle sat forward. It was good to hear excitement in Elliot's voice again. But who was the lucky lady?

"She's bright and beautiful and, best of all, it's someone you know."

Kyle chuckled. That certainly limited the field.

"I can't believe how much I'm looking forward to this."

But who was it?

"And Jeannie seems to be just as pleased as I am."

The empty bottle slipped from his hands. Jeannie?

"We met as I was leaving the gala. We've talked on the phone a few times since then and we're going out for dinner tonight."

Elliot was still talking but Kyle couldn't hear anything over the buzzing inside his head. He only knew one Jeannie. A complicated woman with warm eyes and cool, satiny skin. There was only one Jeannie like that.

"Thanks again for the push, Kyle. I'll let you know how it goes."

"I can hardly wait," he muttered, then stabbed the rewind button and returned to the kitchen. Standing in front of the open fridge, Kyle stared blankly at the shelves.

He slammed the door shut. Jeannie hadn't said a word about seeing Elliot. And why would she? He was the opponent after all. But if she honestly believed Elliot was her ticket to win, she was sadly mistaken.

Elliot was accustomed to a woman with simple wants and a quiet nature. Someone content to sit in the passenger seat, not always compelled to drive.

There was no question in Kyle's mind. Jeannie couldn't possibly be Elliot's type. He might be vulnerable right now, but Elliot was a smart man. It wouldn't take him long to discover that Jeannie was all wrong for him.

Always running, never stopping to listen to reason. All that energy and fire. Kyle pushed a hand through his hair. Elliot didn't stand a chance and she knew it.

Kyle glanced over his shoulder at the answering machine. He owed Elliot a warning, something to give him half a chance before Jeannie had him spinning out of control and ready to say "I do," again.

Kyle shuddered at the idea of playing best man at Jeannie's wedding as he hit the play button again, hoping Elliot had mentioned the bar or a name of a restaurant. "Kyle?"

"I'm here, buddy," Kyle whispered, then turned up the volume, listening to the message all the way through this time and smacking his fist against the wall when no restaurant was named.

The woman was insufferable. All the men in the city and she had to pick on Elliot. But then again, it was only a first date. How much could happen on a first date? A couple of drinks, good food. A kiss good-night.

Kyle groaned. Elliot just wasn't ready for that.

Lifting the receiver, he punched in a number.

She answered on the first ring, her voice low and husky. "Miss me already, baby?"

He smiled. "Not really, Magda, but I do need your help."

"Kyle?" She managed to pull her voice up an octave before speaking again. "What are you doing on my phone?"

"Finding out where Jeannie Renamo is. You were supposed to keep me informed. She's out there with my best friend and I want to know why."

"I tried to stop her. But you know how Jeannie can be."

Only too well. "Where are they?"

"I don't know. She asked me to recommend a couple of restaurants so I told her La Scala has better pasta, but if you want a dessert tray you'll remember for life, then Julie's—"

"Magda?"

"Hmm?"

"Good night."

Less than half an hour later Kyle peered over the maître d's shoulder, hoping for a quick glimpse of the couple he was searching for. "I'm here to meet some friends. They'll be under Daniels or Renamo."

"Daniels?" The maître d' dropped the pen and pointed out the table. "Over there."

Kyle hung back, watching them from the door. It was worse than he had expected. They were looking into each other's eyes, glasses raised in a toast, and Elliot was grinning like an idiot—the same way he had on the day he married Yvonne. Kyle only hoped he wasn't too late.

"Elliot," he called.

"Kyle?" Elliot stood as Kyle approached, but Jeannie stayed fixed to the chair, her eyes narrowing.

"Well, fancy running into you here," Kyle said, looking from one to the other. "I've been meaning to try this place for ages and figured tonight was as good a time as any." He turned to Jeannie. "And how are you?"

"Just fine." She folded her arms and sat back. "I didn't expect you back so soon."

"Obviously not." Kyle smiled at her as he dragged a chair from a neighboring table. "But this certainly is nice," he continued, his knees bumping hers as he sat down. "Just the three of us. Any wine left in that bottle?"

"Have mine," Jeannie said, inching her legs out of the way as she slid her glass toward him. "I've had about enough anyway."

Kyle caught a hint of her perfume as she leaned toward him. He inhaled deeply, quietly. She wore something different again. Something light, fresh. And deadly.

"Why, thank you, Jeannie," he said, lifting the bottle to top up the glass.

"Did you get my message?" Elliot asked.

"Message?" Kyle answered innocently.

"On your machine. I didn't mention my date with Jeannie earlier because I wasn't sure how things would work out. But since you're here, I should thank you for pointing her out to me at the gala. If not for you, we would never have met."

"Don't I know it," Kyle replied, but his eyes were on Jeannie, sitting there so calm and self-assured, as though Elliot was already signed, sealed and delivered.

Kyle shifted his attention to the man he'd come to protect. "You've obviously had a chance to talk then. To find out all about each other."

"Not really," Elliot admitted. "To be honest, most of the talk centered on me."

"I guess Jeannie didn't tell you all about her plans for the future, then." Kyle glanced at Jeannie while he sipped at his wine. She didn't flinch, didn't even blink. She was better than he'd imagined. Or worse, he wasn't sure which anymore.

Elliot smiled at her. "As a matter of fact, we did talk about the future."

"I'll bet you did," Kyle muttered. "And that future didn't happen to include marriage, did it?"

"I'm hoping," Elliot said wistfully. "But I'll know for sure tomorrow."

"Tomorrow?"

"I'll have my answer then."

Kyle slapped the glass down hard. "Elliot, listen to me. You don't know anything about her. You don't know what's behind all of this."

"A good heart, I'd say."

"Or a good line," Kyle countered.

Elliot seemed not to have heard. He reached across the table to take her hand. "It's not often a man meets a woman like Jeannie."

"You're right about that."

"I mean, how many women do you know who would insist on sending a man back to his wife to give it one more try?"

Kyle looked at Jeannie. She said nothing, but Elliot's words hung in the air between them. Kyle turned back to his friend. "What are you saying?"

"Only that Jeannie's convinced me to give my marriage another shot. I'm going to Montreal to talk to Yvonne. If she tells me it's really over herself, I'll let go once and for all. But if there's even the faintest hesitation, I'm going to fight to get her back." He glanced at his watch and stood up. "In fact, we have to leave. I've got a flight to catch and I still have to get Jeannie home."

"There's no time for that," Jeannie told him. "You go on. I'll be fine."

"She's right," Kyle cut in. "You can't risk missing that flight." He wasn't sure of Jeannie's motives for all of this, but the sooner Elliot was in Montreal, the better. "I'll take her home."

Jeannie glanced over at him. "That's a good idea."

Kyle watched her rise from the chair, wondering what the angle was this time. She wrapped her arms around Elliot's neck. "Promise you'll let me know how it goes."

If Kyle hadn't known better, he would have sworn they'd known each other a long time. The affection between them was spontaneous and genuine. And so easy.

Elliot took a step back. "I'll take care of the bill on my way out. And, Kyle, I'll call you when I get back."

He could only nod as his friend walked away.

Jeannie gathered up her purse and slipped on her jacket, taking pains to keep from looking at him. "You heard Elliot's message, didn't you?"

"Yes," Kyle conceded.

"And you came to protect him." She glanced up, her eyes touched with a sadness he could only put down to Elliot's departure. "Well, I hope you weren't too disappointed."

"Jeannie—"

She silenced him with a single glance. "You still don't get it, do you? I'm not just in this for the win. I told you I want a family of my own someday. Finding the right man to share that dream with will be the real prize, Kyle. Taking over your office will simply be the bonus."

She was already at the door by the time he caught up with her. Reaching past her, he grabbed the bar and held the door closed, trapping her between his arms without touching her. If she was to take a single step back, however, or even turn around, everything would change. "I owe you an apology, Jeannie."

"You certainly do." In one quick move, she banged her shoulder against the door, launching them both into the street.

Jeannie felt him catch her, breaking her fall, his hands warm and sure on her shoulders—the very hands she wanted so much to avoid. "I don't need your help," she muttered, shaking him loose.

Humor warmed the blue ice of his eyes. "I can tell."

Turning away while she still could, Jeannie walked to the curb, already cursing herself for letting Elliot get away.

"What are you doing?" Kyle asked.

She raised a hand to flag down a cab. "Going home."

He waved the cab away. "You told Elliot you'd let me take you home."

"I lied."

"Well, I didn't." He took her hand. "Let's go."

"No," Jeannie shouted, but discovered that sexy spikes were not designed to let a woman dig in her heels. It was sit down or follow. She stumbled after him. "Do you have any idea how much I hate it when you do this?"

"I'm sure you'll tell me."

"I hate it so much, I want to scream. I want to scream and smack your arrogant face so hard, it makes your ears ring."

He was too fast, too strong. She was inside the darkened doorway of one of the shops, pinned between his arms with her back against the window before she knew what was happening.

"Then do it," he muttered. "Scream at me. Slap my face. But do something, because if you don't, I will. I can't stand it anymore, Jeannie."

She could feel the heat of his body through the thin silk of her dress, a sharp contrast to the chill of the glass on her back. She shivered as he moved closer, his chest brushing the hard peaks of her breasts with each breath he took.

"When I heard you were with Elliot tonight, I wanted to believe the worst because it makes everything easier for me. You're nothing I've ever wanted, nothing I want now. Yet I've been thinking about you, every hour, every day. And I'm positive you've been thinking about me, too."

Her fingers gripped his jacket, meaning to push him away, but drawing him nearer instead. "You son of a—"

"That's it. Pull me in, Jeannie. Take what you want. What we both want. Maybe that way we can make sense of what's happening."

Headlights from a passing car flashed a harsh white light across his face, showing her for a brief moment the raw, aching need in his eyes. The same need that coiled tighter and tighter inside of her.

"I don't want anything," she breathed. "Not from you."

"No?" Hands that were hard and callused stroked her hair, her face, her throat so lightly, so tenderly, it made her eyes sting. Strong fingers circled the nape of her neck, tilting her head as she knew he liked it, but only the sweet warmth of his breath caressed her lips while he waited for her to bring them together. "Your body is telling me something different."

"Pay no attention," Jeannie whispered even as her arms wound slowly, tentatively around his neck.

"Too late," he murmured. "I've already heard. How can I forget?"

"Like this." Pushing him back hard, Jeannie fled for the curb and the safety of a passing cab, waving her arms and praying it wasn't occupied.

Kyle caught her easily, of course. She hadn't fooled herself that he wouldn't. He spun her around to face him, his eyes dark and searching, his touch compelling, but the cab was waiting and this time she wouldn't let herself be distracted.

With Kyle she felt too much, wanted too much and would eventually give too much. There would be nothing left for herself.

"Let me take you home," he whispered against her hair. "It's the least I can do."

"You're wrong, Kyle." Jeannie opened the cab door and stepped inside. "The least you can do is leave me alone."

8

―――→ ←――

"**P**sst. Wanna see something neat?"

Jeannie turned in the direction of the whisper. Magda stood in the doorway, feet planted wide apart, a voluminous pink jacket clutched close about her.

Jeannie smiled. "I'm almost afraid to say it, but yes."

Magda opened the jacket with a flourish. Splashed across the front of an electric blue T-shirt in bold white letters were the words: Love, Schmuv. He's Rich And I Want Him.

"So, what do you think?" Magda asked.

Jeannie sat back. "I think I want one."

"Who knows you better?" Reaching into one of her pockets, Magda pulled out a second T-shirt, this one the color of ripe pumpkins, and laid it in Jeannie's lap. "The way I see it, if Victoria keeps going the way she is, these babies will be worth a fortune one day."

"Let's hope." Jeannie rose, pulled the T-shirt over her head and smoothed it down over her pants. "How does it look?"

"Fabulous." Magda plopped down in the chair across from her. "So what's Victoria up to this week?"

"She's reached my favorite part. 'Acquiring Expensive Tastes.'"

"Oh, yeah?" Magda twisted Jeannie's monitor around

and scanned the list of essentials. "Caviar," she said, turning the screen back. "You forgot caviar."

"I know." Jeannie sat down and propped her feet up on the desk. "I hate the stuff so I'm leaving it out."

"You can't. Caviar is part of having expensive taste. Like knowing good wine and how to sit a horse."

"I'm not putting horses in, either."

Magda rolled her eyes. "Amateurs." She sniffed and sat back. "So, now that Elliot is gone, what are you planning to do next?"

"Finish the column and then raid your social events file."

Jeannie checked her watch. With a little luck, she could do both and still be gone before Kyle was through with the morning's interviews. That way, she wouldn't have to face him at all.

"There's a gallery opening in Bucktown this week," Magda offered. "But I don't know how good it will be for Victoria."

Jeannie lowered her feet. "Anything's worth a shot. As long as there's no connection to LeeAnne Alexander or anyone else Kyle knows. I told you he showed up at the restaurant, didn't I?"

"You mentioned it."

"I don't know how, but he always manages to show up at the wrong time. Not that there would ever be a right time. Not with Kyle." She pushed the chair back and stood up. "The man's impossible."

"Agreed. So, what happened after Elliot left for the airport?"

Jeannie shuffled some papers on her desk. "I went home."

"Alone?"

"My date left. Remember?"

Magda pursed her lips. "I'm surprised Kyle didn't offer to take you. He's usually funny about things like that."

Jeannie shrugged and carefully stacked the papers one by one. "He offered. I refused."

"Why?"

"Because I didn't want him to, okay?"

"Or maybe you wanted it too much."

"We've been over this before, Magda. Kyle Hunter is not a prospect. He doesn't even want to be."

"Did he tell you that?"

"Yes. I mean no." Jeannie pushed the papers aside and dropped into the chair, wishing she'd never brought Kyle into the conversation at all. "Look, I'll admit I find him attractive."

"Uh-huh."

"Okay. Very attractive. But that doesn't mean I want to have anything to do with him on a personal level." She picked up a pencil and tapped the point against her leg. "The man is a tyrant."

"Granted."

"With absolutely no regard for the views or opinions of others."

"True enough."

"And 'intense' doesn't even begin to describe him."

"Also true," Magda agreed. "So how far has this thing progressed anyway?"

"All right, he kissed me," Jeannie admitted, hating the plaintive tone in her voice.

"And?" Magda pressed.

"And I didn't want it to stop. Okay?"

"Then why did you?"

"Because he's leaving, Magda. What's the point?"

"Things can change."

"Not that." Jeannie pitched the pencil against the wall, stood up, then sat back down again. "Look, Kyle and I are attracted physically, but it stops right there. I'm not what he wants, he's not what I want. End of story.''

''And you really think it's that simple?''

''Why shouldn't it be?'' Jeannie demanded. ''I know there are women who always fall for the wrong man—Victoria gets letters from them all the time. But I'm not one of them, believe me. This 'thing' between Kyle and I can't possibly go any further. I won't allow it.''

But what if it was already too late? she wondered. What if having Kyle Hunter stuck in her heart meant she was already falling in love with him? What then?

Jeannie was on her feet again, pacing back and forth, trying to stay one step ahead of all the questions that had plagued her for days. ''Can we drop this now? Tell me about your trip to Galena instead.''

Magda watched her a moment longer, her expression thoughtful. Then she gave her head a shake and settled back. ''It was wonderful.''

Grateful, Jeannie sat down again. ''Go on.''

''The inn was fabulous, Desmond was magnificent and I think I'm in love.''

''Just like that?''

''Why not? The man loves food and sex, not necessarily in that order, and thinks of me as voluptuous. Can't get enough of me, in fact. What more could I ask?''

Jeannie managed a smile. ''Nothing at all.''

Food and sex and wanting each other more than anything else. Love was so basic to Magda. No wonder she thought it could work with herself and Kyle.

She stretched her smile wider. ''Sounds like Desmond is a candidate for number four. I'm happy for you.''

''So am I.'' Magda's face softened in a way Jeannie had never seen before. ''It's been so long since I felt this way, I'd forgotten what it's like. But now that I've found it, I'm not about to let go.'' Her hand on Jeannie's was gentle and reassuring. "I deserve this, Jeannie. And so do you."

Kyle's words played over in her mind. *Take what you want. What we both want.* And if she had? If she'd simply stopped fighting long enough to let his passion wash over her, what then? The answer was simple. It would have been the worst mistake of her life.

She pulled away from Magda. "You're absolutely right. I do deserve it. Now all I have to do is find it."

Resigned, Magda waved a hand then stood up. "So come by and go through the social events file. I'm here until five."

The receptionist's voice on the intercom interrupted them. "Magda, front desk please."

"I'll talk to you later." Magda reached out and tapped a fingernail on the monitor. "Caviar and horses. Trust me."

As Magda swept out of her office, Jeannie read the list over one last time, typed *caviar* at the bottom and hit Save. "But no horses," she insisted, and ejected the disk.

Jeannie was only a few steps from Kyle's office when she spotted Magda running toward her. Jeannie could only stare. Magda in full flight was a sight to behold.

"Come with me," she ordered, steadying herself with a hand on the wall while she caught her breath.

Jeannie held up the disk. "I'll just deliver this."

"That can wait. The man in reception won't."

Curious, Jeannie slipped the disk into her pocket and followed Magda back to reception. "Who is it anyway?"

"Stuart Singleton. Recognize the name?"

"Who wouldn't? Airlines, fiber optics—"

"And charity in a big way. His parents started the Big River Foundation years ago."

"I remember them," Jeannie said. "Scrawny necks, yards of chiffon and a penchant for champagne. They were always in the papers."

"You've got it. And now that Stuart's in charge of the foundation, he seems bent on outdoing them. He's well on his way to becoming the country's foremost philanthropist."

Jeannie smiled. "Sort of a Mother Theresa in drag?"

Magda stopped cold. "Look, Jeannie, this guy has it all. Money, charm and commitment. Don't make me regret coming all the way back here to get you."

"Sorry," Jeannie said sincerely. Magda meant well. But the idea of a man making celebrity balls his life's work struck her as ludicrous. And chiffon had never looked good on her. For Magda's sake, however, Jeannie dutifully fell into step behind her. "What's he doing here?"

"I don't know yet. He was talking to the receptionist when I saw him, so I slipped out before he noticed me." At the end of the hall, Magda turned to Jeannie again. "Now smile, for God's sake. And get rid of that T-shirt."

Jeannie tugged the shirt over her head, stashed it behind a drooping ficus and smiled, but was still unconvinced—until the man standing in reception turned toward them.

He wore faded jeans and a denim shirt with the sleeves rolled up, revealing tanned, sinewy forearms. Thick brown hair was tied back from a face that was too narrow to be really attractive, emphasizing eyes that were dark and watchful.

But his mouth…oh, his mouth. Full on the bottom and a perfect Cupid's bow on the top. The kind of mouth that should be held up as the standard by which all male mouths were measured.

He stared for a moment, then a smile spread slowly across his face. The transformation was breathtaking. Where he'd seemed closed and forbidding only a moment ago, this brooding Heathcliff in blue jeans now seemed warm and approachable. The sort of man who would instinctively hate chiffon.

"Magda," he said, his voice a husky half whisper that drew Jeannie immediately.

She waited as the two embraced, already feeling her mind opening. The next hurdle was the heart. A tiny crack would do it. She broadened her smile as Magda introduced them.

"Stuart, this is one of our writers, Jeannie Renamo. Jeannie, this is Stuart Singleton."

Jeannie extended her hand. "It's a pleasure." His hand was knobby and hard, meaning the work clothes were real. So far so good.

"Will I have read any of your work in the magazine?" he asked, those watchful eyes on her alone now.

"I hope not," Magda mumbled, "Stuart, would you mind if Jeannie joined us? She's doing some research on charity organizations and I thought it might help if she sat in."

"Not at all," Stuart replied.

"Wonderful," Magda said, as she linked her arm with him and led them into the boardroom. "I can't tell you how good it is see you again."

"It's been too long," he agreed, and Jeannie couldn't detect anything insincere—another point in his favor.

"Now tell me you haven't gone and done anything that would break my heart," Magda crooned. "Like getting married."

"I haven't had time to think about it." Stuart's dark gaze settled on Jeannie again as they sat down. "But there's always the possibility of change."

Magda shot her a glance so heavy with meaning, it should have fallen on the table between them. But Jeannie caught it in time. "Magda tells me you're one of this country's foremost philanthropists. A Mother Theresa in...blue jeans."

He gave a self-mocking laugh that Jeannie quite liked. "Magda flatters me. I just do what I can."

"Nonsense," Magda protested. "This man has done more to promote charities worldwide than anyone I know."

"But this time I'm working a little closer to home," he said solemnly. "Which is why I'm here. There's a youth rehab center in Alaska that needs a boost, so I'm planning a fund-raiser to get things rolling."

"A gala on ice?" Jeannie quipped.

Stuart laughed softly, taking her gibe in stride. "I'm afraid I'm not really good at galas, Jeannie. What I have in mind is more of a retreat at the ranch."

"Ranch?"

"Yes," Magda cut in. "The kind with horses."

"Some," Stuart agreed. "But mostly good Montana heifers. There'll be plenty of food, entertainment and good company."

"Sounds like fun," Jeannie offered.

"Not all of it. Some of the most widely recognized minds in addiction research will also be there for open seminars. I'm hoping it will also be a learning opportunity. For those who want it, of course."

Jeannie leaned forward, interested. "I've never heard of anything like this."

"That's because I like to do things quietly." He smiled at Magda. "If all goes well, it'll be something like the Rainforest Weekend we did years ago, remember?"

"How could I forget? I had a three-toed sloth for a dinner partner. Nasty thing kept trying to put his head in my lap all evening. Or was that the senator? I always mix them up."

Stuart laughed again. "I promise, no animals this time. Political or otherwise. Just friends and concerned individuals. Which is why I'm here. I need your help."

"Anything," Magda said.

"I need discreet press coverage once it's over. No advance publicity, no unauthorized photographs. I've always counted on you in the past, Magda, and I'm hoping I can this time, as well."

"Name the date."

"Next weekend. Friday to Sunday. I know it's short notice, but we weren't even sure it was a go until a few days ago."

Magda clicked her tongue. "Oh, Stuart, I'm sorry, but I'm booked." She brightened, as if struck by sudden inspiration. "But maybe Jeannie could go."

Focusing on the cause and the man, Jeannie lowered her lashes and smiled. "I'd be honored."

"Wonderful," Stuart said, his voice dipping into that husky whisper Jeannie so enjoyed. "Why don't I arrange transportation for you?"

"I wouldn't want to put you to any trouble."

"You won't be. But I will need your number."

They stopped by Jeannie's desk as they walked to the elevator and she handed Stuart her card.

"I'm looking forward to seeing you again," he said, his gaze skimming over her, showing appreciation without leering—a rare skill, Jeannie acknowledged.

"Me, too," Jeannie said honestly. Stuart was intelligent, committed to what he believed in and unattached. The kind of man she always liked to meet. The fact that he was filthy rich only made him more suitable now.

The elevator opened. Stuart held the door while a harried deliveryman wrestled a cloud of helium balloons out of the car and over to reception. Red, orange, green, blue—Jeannie couldn't think of a color that wasn't there.

Stuart smiled at her as he stepped into the elevator. "Until next weekend, then."

"So what do you think?" Magda asked as the door slid shut.

"I think I'm going to have to add horses to my list,"

Jeannie said. And her heart would just have to learn to like it.

"Jeannie Renamo?" the deliveryman called.

"That's me," she answered, and he thrust the knotted ribbons into her hand.

"Sign here, please," he said, then handed her a small square envelope. "Enjoy."

Magda watched over Jeannie's shoulder as she slit the seal on the envelope. Inside was a plain white card with a single line: "No more wondering. Thanks, Yvonne and Elliot."

Jeannie smiled as she folded the card back into the envelope. "Ha, I was right."

"Wonderful," Magda said. "But right now we have to talk strategy. How about Asti's for lunch?"

"Fine." Jeannie motioned to the balloons. "I'll just tie these up somewhere."

"I'll take them for you," Kyle offered.

Jeannie drew in a deep breath and turned around, annoyed that the sound of his voice already had her heart pounding. He came toward her, his blue gaze steady, revealing nothing.

"Thanks," she said, focusing on the balloons. "They're from Yvonne and Elliot. Seems everything worked out fine."

"I know. Elliot called about an hour ago."

Her gaze slipped back to him, watching as his lips curved in one of those rare, broad grins that deepened his dimples and made her smile in spite of herself.

Kyle's mouth was far from perfect, Jeannie realized. His lips were too thin and his usual expression grim, drawing the corners of his mouth down, often making him appear stern and hard. But when that mouth was on hers, it came to life—playing her, consuming her, making her open to all the passion that burned within him.

Which was exactly the problem, she reminded herself.

That inexplicable pull she felt every time he was near. The only solution was to get as far away from it as possible. And somewhere like Montana would do nicely.

"I'm happy for them," Kyle said. "But their timing couldn't be worse. Elliot's decided to stay in Montreal for a while, which leaves me shorthanded for the race next week."

"Race?" Jeannie asked.

"The sailing race in Bristol Harbor. Starts on Monday and goes all week. It's not the America's Cup, but it's fun. And with a proper crew, we stand a pretty good chance."

"Only, now you're short one man. What will you do?"

Kyle shrugged. "Something will work out. If not, I can get by with three."

But the deep furrow between his brows made Jeannie wonder.

He motioned to the balloons. "You'd better give those to me if you want to get anywhere near a table at Asti's." He took the ribbons from her. "I'd like to talk to you when you get back."

"I'm not coming back," Jeannie said too quickly, then tried to cover with a smile. "I have plans. Research to do."

"I only want to go over something with you," he said softly. "But it can wait until tomorrow."

She watched him walk away, waiting for the rush of relief that should have come with knowing she'd managed to push him away once and for all. But there was only that same tug deep inside her, and a longing she couldn't explain.

"Pity about his crew," Magda whispered.

"I hope he finds someone," Jeannie said absently.

"I hear LeeAnne Alexander is quite a sailor. Maybe she'll go."

"Probably."

"Of course, he won't really need anyone very experienced for a fourth. Just someone who can pull a rope and move fast."

"Well, I gave up jogging a long time ago, so you can stop right there," Jeannie warned. "He didn't ask and I'm not about to volunteer."

Magda snatched the envelope from Jeannie's hand and pulled out the note. "'No more wondering,'" she read. "Interesting concept."

"It has absolutely no bearing in this situation."

Magda handed back the note. "Too bad. If nothing else, Race Week is the perfect time to meet rich men from up and down the coast. A golden opportunity as it were. I'm sure Victoria wouldn't want to miss it."

"Victoria is going to be too busy learning how to ride and tend cattle," Jeannie countered. "She won't have time to think about sailboats."

Magda hit the elevator button. "I give up. Are you coming to lunch?"

"I forgot my purse," Jeannie said, then dashed across the lobby. "Wait one second."

Kyle's secretary, Trish, a wispy blonde he had inherited from Marcus, smiled as Jeannie walked by. "How's the search going?"

"Great," Jeannie lied. "I expect to be announcing wedding plans anyday now."

"I hope so," Trish said, "because everyone is talking about Victoria Boulderbottom. I hear them at the Laundromat, at the clubs—everywhere. She can't let them down."

"Has she ever?" Jeannie pulled the disk from the pocket. "By the way. Can you give this to Kyle? It's the next instalment."

"Of course." Trish reached out with eager hands.

"But can I have a look first? I'm dying to know what comes next."

"As long as it gets to him eventually," Jeannie said, then continued on to her office.

Grabbing her purse from the drawer, she headed back along the hall to Reception. Trish gave her two thumbs-up as she passed. "Oh, I meant to tell you," she called out. "Since I've been monitoring the calls and letters that come in for Victoria—"

Jeannie froze. "Monitoring?" she cut in. "I was under the impression that all my calls and mail still came to me."

"They do," Trish assured her. "The receptionist just kind of routes them through here first so I can do an informal survey. You know, how many hope Victoria finds herself a rich man, how many hope she falls flat on her face... That kind of thing. So far we're running six to one in her favor."

Jeannie concentrated on keeping her tone light. "That's wonderful. And who authorized this?"

"Kyle, of course. He probably just forgot to tell you. Anyway, he's also arranged to have the question in next week's issue with a special telephone number printed beside it. As of Monday, one of the incoming lines will be dedicated to answering those calls on a machine, so the whole process will be streamlined."

"Really?" Jeannie said, almost choking with the effort to keep her voice down. How many others knew about this? she wondered.

"Oh, yeah," Trish went on. "He's got really big plans for cashing in on this thing. Billboards, newspapers, the whole nine yards. But then, I guess you know all that."

Jeannie managed a smile. She wasn't about to admit this was the first she'd heard of it. An open discussion would have been too much to expect from Kyle, but a passing reference would have been nice.

Anger and bitterness twisted her stomach. Regardless of what Magda or her own heart might think, there was nothing at all for her to wonder about or regret where Kyle was concerned.

Trish's phone rang—two short chirps meaning an internal call. She punched the speaker button. "Trish Chamber's desk."

Kyle's voice sounded hollow and distant. "Trish, did you get that quarterly report yet?"

"Sure did. I'll bring it in."

She reached for the report on her tray but Jeannie's hand was there first. "Why don't I take it for you? That way, you can continue to read."

Trish beamed. "Thanks."

"Oh, and could you just call reception and let Magda know I'll be a while?"

"No problem," Trish replied.

Jeannie didn't bother to knock as she entered the office. "Kyle, I want to talk to you."

He laid down his pen as she closed the door. "I thought you were going to lunch."

"I changed my mind." She dropped her purse and the quarterly report on the credenza. "I've just heard that my calls are being routed through Trish. And I want to know why." Jeannie advanced slowly, gaining strength from the sound of her own voice. "I also want to know why I wasn't included in the plans to exploit the series with billboards, print ads and God knows what else." She rested both hands on the desk. "I want some answers, Kyle. And I want them now."

His eyes were like ice. "Let me remind you that you're not a partner yet, Jeannie."

"But I am Victoria Boulderbottom," she said with quiet conviction. "And I have the right to know what's going on."

Kyle considered a moment, then pushed a folder toward her. "This should tell you everything you need to know."

Jeannie floundered for a moment, her anger suddenly without focus. Then she spun the folder around and flipped back the cover. In front of her were pages of notes outlining an advertising campaign for Victoria Boulderbottom. Billboards, newspaper, radio—everything Trish had mentioned and more. But it didn't appear as though anything concrete had been done yet. The idea was still in the planning stages.

She sat down, taking the file into her lap so she could go through it page by page. *How very clever,* she thought. With this kind of exposure, there would be even more pressure for Victoria to win, and Kyle knew it. He was upping the ante one more time.

She closed the folder and set it on his desk. "You were wrong to keep this from me."

"I can understand why you'd feel that way," he said matter-of-factly. "But now that you've seen it, I'd like to know what you think."

"First, I want to know how long you've been working on it."

"Since the day we made the bet."

"And how many people know about it?"

"You're number three."

Jeannie ignored the relief spreading through her. "What you're planning is going to cost a fortune."

"That's true, but the return will be worth it. I figure 'Marrying Well' is going to peak in about six weeks. After that, Victoria will lose momentum, and audience, unless she's well on her way to a wedding day. It doesn't leave much time, but the campaign is carefully targeted to give us the most immediate and dramatic hit possible. If all goes well, women will start reading *Aspects* for Victoria, and hopefully stay with us after she's gone." He gestured at the file. "What do you think?"

Jeannie traced a fingertip along the edge of the folder. "It's brilliant. But why have you sat on it so long?"

"Because of the pressure it will put on you."

"Don't worry about that. This is just what Victoria needs."

"But is it what you need?" he asked gently. "Believe it or not, I wouldn't have gone any further without speaking to you about it. And if you'd prefer we hold off, or don't run it at all, I'll understand."

"Because you still don't think I can do it?"

"Because I'm afraid you will do it."

"Is the idea of my being your partner that frightening?"

"Not at all. It's the thought of you marrying someone to win that's frightening."

"I wouldn't do that."

"You say that now." He motioned to the file. "But how will you feel when the pressure really heats up?"

Jeannie shrugged, feigning a confidence she didn't feel. "The advertising won't make much difference to me. I plan to win anyway. You're the one who'll notice a difference. This campaign will give your new format the foothold it needs before you have to leave. The timing couldn't be more perfect."

Kyle nodded. "That's exactly what I thought."

She leaned forward. "So when do we start?"

"If you're sure it's what you want, then it has to be right away. Unfortunately I'm leaving for Maine in a few hours and I'll be gone all week. But we can work by fax and modem. It'll mean a bit of juggling and a loss of spontaneity, but I can't see a way around it." He paused. "Unless you come with me."

"Kyle, that's impossible—"

"Just hear me out," he interrupted. "The race doesn't start until Monday. We'd be finished by then, and you could be back in Chicago to put everything in motion."

"I don't know."

"Jeannie, I'm asking you to come as a colleague on a business trip, nothing more. However, if you don't feel comfortable with the arrangement, we'll make do with the fax and a modem. The choice is yours."

Jeannie hesitated. Why was she even thinking about this? She had what she wanted. Why upset the balance now?

Because the campaign and Race Week would be a good opportunity for Victoria, she reasoned. All those rich men with their fancy yachts, just waiting for someone to go below with them. Think of the column it would make.

"I'll go," she told him. "But not for two days. I want to stay till Friday. I want to be the fourth on your crew."

"Don't be ridiculous. You don't know anything about sailing."

"I'll learn," she said evenly. "There must be something fairly basic I can do. Something like pulling a rope and moving fast."

"That's basic, all right."

She lifted her chin. "And it's the only way I'll go. Take it or leave it."

Kyle studied her closely. "I guess I'll take it, on one condition. I'll give you a chance to learn the basics, as you call it. But if you don't catch on quickly enough, you're gone first thing Monday morning."

"And who'll judge my progress?"

"I will. Take it or leave it."

"I guess I'll take it."

"Now all I want to know is why."

"That's easy." Jeannie crossed to the credenza. "Race Week attracts rich men from up and down the coast— everyone knows that." She glanced back at him. "Victoria wouldn't miss it for the world."

A wry smile curved the corners of his lips. "I should have known."

"Yes," she said softly. "You should have." Kyle made no reply and Jeannie was the first to turn away. "Now all I need is the name of a hotel."

"Nothing will be available now. You'll have to stay at my house." He held up a hand when she started to protest. "I'll be staying on the boat anyway. Believe me, Jeannie, I heard every word you said last night, and you have nothing to worry about. I'll leave you alone."

She nodded. "Okay, then, it's settled. When do we leave?"

"Six o'clock tonight. We'll change planes in Boston and then drive out from Bangor. It'll be a long night, so dress comfortably and be sure to pack some warm clothing for the boat. It can get cold out on the water this time of year."

"Fine." Jeannie walked to his desk and picked up the file. "Mind if I take this with me? I want to go over the campaign in more detail before we leave."

"It's yours." He took a thick paperback from his bottom drawer and tossed it to her. "Take this, too."

She turned it around. *"The Sailor's Handbook?"*

Kyle stood up and opened the door for her. "You're going to need all the help you can get."

9

Jeannie stood in the doorway of Kyle's bedroom, tapping *The Sailor's Handbook* against her leg and trying not to laugh.

Less than ten paces away, a huge mahogany sleigh bed awaited her—crisp, white sheets already turned back and a single rose positioned on one of the oversize pillows.

A bouquet of lilacs, the tiny flowers still tightly closed, scented the room with a sweet, heady perfume, and from somewhere came the soft strains of a flute concerto. On each nightstand, candles flickered inside hurricane glasses while a couple of logs smoldered on the grate behind the fireplace doors. The only thing missing was a bottle of wine and a smoking jacket.

Hearing Kyle's footsteps on the stairs, Jeannie stepped back into the hall.

"Didn't you find your room?" he asked, nodding at the bag still on her shoulder.

"Oh, I found it." She smiled and pushed the door open for him. "It was kind of hard to miss."

Kyle stared at the scene before him, then groaned. "I don't believe this." He then flicked on the lights.

Jeannie watched with amusement as he blew out the candles. "Your housekeeper is well trained, I see."

"No," he said emphatically then plucked the rose

from the pillow and jammed it in with the lilacs. "Just misguided."

"You mean she doesn't do this for all the girls?"

Kyle shot her a warning glance. "She doesn't get the chance." But there was humor in those icy blues and she could see he was having trouble holding back a smile as he dropped the bags in front of the armoire.

"Dorothy's been trying to marry me off for the longest time," he explained, "but I think she was running out of candidates. When I told her I was bringing a woman with me, she must have been overjoyed, and decided to help things along."

"Well, she certainly thought of everything." Jeannie plunked her duffel bag beside the fireplace. "It's just a pity she went to all this trouble for nothing."

"We could change that if you like."

His eyebrows danced up and down in the most absurd leer she'd ever seen. "In your dreams," she said, laughing.

"As always." He sighed and opened the armoire. "There's lots of room in here, and there should be a couple of empty drawers in the dresser."

"What if I prefer to sleep in the guest room?"

Kyle shrugged and crossed over to the fireplace. "Sheets are in the linen closet. Help yourself. But that room's still under construction, so try not to trip over the power saws when you turn out the light." Kneeling down, he opened the glass doors and poked at the logs. "Besides, I can assure you my bed is the more comfortable of the two."

"I'm sure it is."

"And warmer."

She walked over to stand beside him. "Okay, you've convinced me. Which side do you sleep on?"

He glanced up. "The right."

"Then I'll be sure to stick to the left."

He smacked at her feet and Jeannie leapt up onto the sofa behind him, laughing as she sank back against the cushions. When he turned back to the fire, Jeannie tucked her feet safely underneath her and took a good look around.

Her dislike of antiques didn't keep her from appreciating the beauty of Kyle's furnishings. Nor from acknowledging how right they were for this house.

Jeannie had envisioned finding a glass-and-steel palace at the end of his long, winding driveway. Instead, she'd been greeted by an old clapboard farmhouse set high on a rocky knoll overlooking the harbor, all the windows ablaze with welcoming light—the kind of house where she expected to hear the slam of a screen door at any minute, or see an old tire swing hanging from a tree. A house more suited to a family than a man living alone.

Jeannie stretched her arms along the back of the sofa. "Why does your housekeeper want to marry you off so badly?"

Kyle finished separating the logs, effectively putting an end to Dorothy's fire. "She's worried about this trip I'm planning," he said, then closed the doors and shut off the air intake. "She's convinced I need someone to keep me company, to look after me. Hence, the romantic interlude." He smiled as he got to his feet. "A little overdone, but from the heart."

"And if you had been planning the interlude," Jeannie said as he settled into the opposite corner of the sofa, "where would you have drawn the line?"

"No candles to start with."

"Too bad. The candles were my favorite part."

"Okay, candles. But no fire."

"No fire?"

"All right then, what would you leave out?"

"The flute concerto," she said without hesitation. "Soft rock would be my aphrodisiac of choice."

He made no reply, simply watched her for a long moment, the promise in his eyes holding her still, unable to turn away.

"I'll keep that in mind," he said at last, and Jeannie realized that was exactly what she wanted. To have him play the music and light the candles for her. And to have him touch her, now, while the fire still glowed.

She reached down and unzipped her duffel bag. "Shall we go over the Boulderbottom campaign for a few minutes?"

"Don't you think we should get some sleep?"

She set the folder on her lap. "I don't think I could sleep right away. But if you want to get going, that's okay. You drove, I didn't."

"I'm okay for a while." He laced his fingers behind his neck and closed his eyes. "But I don't want to think too much. How about we just talk?"

"About what?"

"Anything. Where you went to school, the first time you fell in love. Anything."

Jeannie dropped the file on the floor. "Holy Rosary, grade six, Steven Mueller. He had red hair and freckles, and he made me laugh. He used to ride his bike past my house and fall on the lawn so I'd run out and see if he was hurt. Then we'd sit on the curb and he'd tell me jokes. New ones every day. He was amazing."

"Sounds serious."

"Very. Which was the problem. You see, Steven was an older man. Grade seven."

"Ah, a bad influence."

"Exactly. So when my brother threatened to beat him up the next time he came around, I started sneaking over to his house instead. But it wasn't the same. Poor Steven was always looking over his shoulder, wondering if Pauli was coming after him, and it wasn't long before I discovered him falling on some other girl's lawn.''

"So you risked your brother's wrath for naught."

"Sad but true," Jeannie said on a sigh. "I was heartbroken, of course."

"I'm not surprised. And does your brother still protect you from bad influences?"

"No, thank God," she said, smiling broadly. "He's too far away."

"That's right. You told me he was up for a recording contract. How did it go?"

"Not well. Apparently, negotiations broke down over 'artistic differences,' and Pauli was out the door." Jeannie sighed and stretched out her legs. "It's not the first time, either. That man is so stubborn. He'd rather risk his entire career than compromise."

"Sounds like a brave man," Kyle offered.

"Or foolish."

"Must be a family trait." He smiled when she turned to him. "The bravery. Not the foolishness. I've never met a woman less afraid of anything than you."

Jeannie very nearly laughed, because at that moment she was very afraid. Of the compassion in his eyes, the warmth in his touch and the need to feel that warmth surrounding her.

Her gaze strayed to the bed and she was suddenly jealous of every woman who had ever been in this room before her, every woman who hadn't been afraid to want him, to love him.

She rose and walked to the door. "It's late. You should be getting back to the boat. Sailing lessons start early."

Kyle followed her down the stairs. "I'll pick you up at seven o'clock. You have my number at the marina in case you need anything."

"I won't," Jeannie assured him as they walked out to the porch. "Good night."

Back in his room, Jeannie laid her nightshirt on the bed and shed her clothes slowly, letting her jeans slide down over her hips and legs, the worn denim soft against her feet as she stepped out of them. She dropped her sweater beside them, slipped the nightshirt over her head and tossed all but one of Kyle's pillows onto the floor. Then she slid between the sheets, fully prepared to spend a fitful night in a strange house, and even stranger bed.

But Kyle's sleigh bed proved to be warm and deep. Within minutes, Jeannie was drifting on the edge of sleep, snuggled under his duvet on the right side of the bed.

Jeannie's head popped through the hatch again. "I found the wine, but I can't find a corkscrew."

Kyle raised his head. "Don't worry about it. I'll be finished with this sail in a minute, then I'll come and look."

She came up into the sunshine, the bulky coat and pants she'd worn all morning abandoned in favor of a pair of shorts and cropped T-shirt, the color of the afternoon sky.

The wind's chill was gone now that they were anchored in a sheltered bay, and Kyle watched her raise her arms, stretching like a cat in the sun, her movements so unconsciously graceful and feminine that she took his breath away and left his heart pounding in his chest.

She turned and moved toward him, crossing the deck as nimbly as any experienced sailor. From the moment she'd stepped on board, Kyle had known Jeannie was a natural. She'd been everywhere, anxious to learn, and more importantly, to understand.

The true test had come, however, when they were finally underway, a moment which he knew quickly separated those who would fall in love with the sea from those who would merely endure.

Hoping to discourage her from wanting to join the crew, Kyle had immediately taken the boat to windward, making her heel over at a severe angle. But Jeannie's shriek had been one of pure delight as she sat clinging to the rails. And once they leveled out, she'd been on her feet again, developing a sense of the wind and the motion instead of fighting it, her laughter real and refreshing, washing over him like gentle waves.

But Kyle hadn't let up on her. All morning he had tacked and jibed, taking the ship through an imaginary course over and over again, hoping to exhaust not only her energy but also her stubborn spirit.

But even cold and shivering, there had been no stopping Jeannie Renamo. And Kyle had been forced to admire her strength even as it frustrated him.

Now, however, she bore little resemblance to the tight-lipped woman who had declared a time-out and had headed below as soon as the anchor was set. Right now, she was all soft curves, warm eyes and long, golden legs.

Kyle deliberately lowered his eyes and concentrated on the task at hand, knowing with grim certainty that it was going to be a very long week.

She swung around the mast and stood beside him. "So when will I meet the rest of the crew?"

"Tomorrow. We'll be running a trial first thing in the morning."

"Do they know I'll be joining you?"

"Not yet. I thought it might be wiser to wait and see how things went today first."

"And how did things go?"

"I'm still deciding. Why don't you explain what I'm doing here to help me make up my mind?"

"No problem." Her lips curved in a smug smile. "First you doused the main so we could anchor."

"Uh-huh."

"Now you're securing the sail to the boom with..."

He glanced up. The smile was gone.

"With what?" he pressed.

"With uh..."

Grinning, he dangled one of the cords in front of her. "With what, Jeannie?"

"The things," she yelled, snatching it from him. "The little things that hold the sail in place." She twisted the cord around the boom, then spun around and headed back to the cockpit.

"Shock cords," Kyle said quietly.

She stopped but didn't turn around. "I knew that."

"Jeannie."

She twisted her head. "What now?"

"You did well today."

"I knew that, too." She smiled again, her lips parting just a little. "Does that mean I'm part of the crew?"

"Do I have a choice?"

"No."

Kyle laughed, watching her strut across the deck as she came back to him. She stood on the opposite side of the boom, but still he could catch the faintest trace of her scent—something different again. Green and woodsy. He inhaled deeply, instinctively. It suited her, yet left him vaguely frustrated and annoyed at his own weakness.

Why couldn't she stick to just one? A single scent that would define her and give him comfort in knowing what to expect, instead of leaving him wondering and always curious.

"I've been thinking about the name problem again," she said, interrupting his misery.

Kyle shook his head. She'd been tossing out names for his boat all morning, each one progressively worse.

"How about *Wood Slivers?*"

"*Wood Slivers?*"

"Wasn't it Duncan who said you prefer the lure of wood slivers to the charms of the city?" She spread her arms wide. "This is the lure of *Wood Slivers.*"

Her smile was almost enough to convince him. "I'll think about it." He finished securing the sail then stepped past her. "But I'm not fond of anything that will bring Duncan Fox to mind."

"I can understand that." She sighed and followed him to the cockpit. Standing by the wheel, she shaded her eyes with her hands as she looked down the length of the boat. "It just seems a shame to call anything as magnificent as this by a number."

Kyle followed her gaze. MT5-6400 was thirty-six feet of steel, teak and fiberglass, every board laid by his own hands or those of men he trusted, every fitting chosen with care. She was his life, his joy, his saving grace. But "magnificent" was not a word he would have used to describe her.

Sound, perhaps, and definitely strong. She rose nicely on the swells, moved well in light airs and steered easily. But more importantly she was good tempered. She followed his lead, responded to his touch and Kyle trusted her with his life.

And Jeannie was right. She was bloody magnificent.

"She'll have a name before I leave in September. The right one," Kyle promised, and was surprised that after nearly two years, the issue should feel important all of a sudden. He motioned to Jeannie. "Come on. Let's find that corkscrew."

She ducked down the companionway ahead of him and reached up to grab two glasses from the overhead cupboard. Kyle tried not to stare at the expanse of creamy skin between her waistband and the raised edge of her T-shirt. Told himself not to follow the hollow of her spine down to where it disappeared into her shorts. Reminded himself that the safest place he could be right now was outside.

She opened the fridge, bending down so her bottom was thrust out just at the level of his hands, then stood up just in time, waving the wine bottle and making him smile.

Finding himself in no hurry to leave all of a sudden, Kyle switched on the radio and fiddled with the dials, bringing in soft rock from somewhere.

Her eyes narrowed as she set the bottle on the table.

"Coincidence," he told her, but didn't change the station.

Kyle found the corkscrew, opened the bottle and poured them both a glass. "Cheers."

Jeannie lightly touched her glass to his, her smile warm. "Do you know what I like best about sailing?" she asked as she settled back against the counter. "The way the water laughs at us. As though it knows something we don't."

Kyle sipped thoughtfully. All he heard was the water lapping at the sides of the boat, telling him the breeze was gentle, the kind that just ruffled the surface of the water. But beyond that, nothing. "What are you talking about?"

"Close your eyes," she urged, "and listen."

Kyle closed his eyes.

"Hear it?"

It was laughter, soft and low. He had never noticed it before.

She flashed him a grin. "Told you." Opening the fridge again, she lifted out the plate of cheese and crack-

ers she'd insisted on making that morning, setting it on
the table in front of him. "I can't get over how cozy it
is in here. Not at all the cramped dark cave I thought it
would be."

"Believe me," Kyle said, laughing. "After a while, it
can begin to feel like a cave. Which is why I had the
cabinets and trim changed to white this spring. I'll need
all the comfort I can get on this next trip."

"Well," she said, taking a bag of grapes from the
fridge, "it certainly did the trick."

While she rinsed the fruit, Kyle looked around the
room that would be his home for the next few years. He
knew every nook and handhold by heart and could walk
through in the dark without bruising a shin.

But there was a different feel to the cabin this afternoon. Warmer somehow. Maybe even cozy, as Jeannie
had suggested. Unconsciously, he looked at her, then deliberately turned away again. The new color scheme was
working, he told himself. It was amazing how much difference a splash of white could make.

"You're really serious about this trip, aren't you?"
Jeannie asked. The change in her tone was subtle, the
edge slight, drawing Kyle back to her.

"Did you think I was kidding?"

Jeannie plucked a small stem of grapes from the bunch.
"No, it just seems like such a lonely thing to do."

"There's a difference between being alone and being
lonely, Jeannie. I've been alone most of my life, but I'm
rarely lonely."

She tucked the grapes between the wedges of cheese,
arranging and rearranging them while she considered his
answer. "What if something goes wrong?" she said at
last.

"Things can go wrong anywhere."

"But on land there's usually someone around to help."

She lifted her gaze to the porthole. "Out there, there's no one." She gave the grapes one last poke, then crossed to the navigation table. "I guess I just can't understand why you want to do it. I see the charts with names likes Azores and Antilles, and I think yes, that's exciting. Then I stand in the cockpit with the sun on my face and the wind at my back, and it's such a feeling of freedom, that I think I could keep going forever, too."

She turned abruptly and took hold of the safety harness attached to the stove. "But then I remember this, or the one upstairs that will keep you from being washed overboard in a storm, and I realize how dangerous it all is." She released the harness and let out a long sigh, her gaze finally meeting his. "And what about hurricanes, accidents, even pirates for God's sake? Don't you think about any of those things, Kyle? Don't you worry at all?"

He watched the harness swing back and forth, the buckle banging against the stove with each pass. "I think about all those things and more, all the time." He reached out, stilling the harness before meeting her gaze. "So I prepare for bad weather and try to avoid accidents. As for pirates..." He shrugged. "I carry a gun and pray I don't have to use it."

Jeannie's face paled. "You're serious about that, too, aren't you?"

"I have to be," Kyle said quietly.

"Then why do it?"

It was a question he heard so often, his reply was automatic. "Adventure, excitement—"

She shook her head. "Not good enough."

Kyle looked at her for a long time, seeing the steel beneath the warmth in those caramel eyes. He should have known better than to try the stock answers with her. She wasn't the type to let him off easily. And for once, there didn't seem to be a good reason to keep trying.

"To fulfill a dream," he said softly. "Something you should understand all too well."

Her fingertips brushed his cheek, the unexpected touch burning him as thoroughly as any seductive caress, making the blood hum in his ears.

On impulse, he took hold of her hand, and she froze, not breaking the contact, yet not moving nearer, either. He felt her fingers tighten fractionally on his, watched the rise and fall of her breasts beneath the T-shirt as her breath quickened soundlessly.

Still he waited, feeling the clench in his groin that urged him to help her decide, the response as uncontrollable as it was unwelcome. Had she been any other woman, he would have saved them both the agony and simply led her to his room at the end of the cabin. But as much as he wanted to, he would not be the one to break their bargain. Not this time.

"Jeannie," he whispered, the single word echoing in the sudden silence of the cabin. She lifted only her eyes to him, the pupils now dark and round. Kyle rubbed his thumb across her palm, watched her lips part.

She would taste of wine and salt air if he kissed her now, deeply the way he wanted to; feeling that sharp tongue against his own, stroking, battling, inviting him in.

He brought her hand to his lips. "I want you, Jeannie," he murmured, brushing feathery kisses across her fingertips, her palm, her wrist, where her pulse beat fast and urgent.

"No." She pushed him back. "I can't."

Kyle held her fast. "Can't with me. Or with anyone?"

Their eyes met and held. "With you."

He released her and walked the length of the cabin. Despite all of his work, it felt pretty cramped in there now. Her jeans and coat were sprawled across his bed, her bag was open on the navigation desk and he couldn't even get out to the cockpit without touching her as he passed. She'd invaded the one place that been his sanctuary and turned everything upside down.

"Watch her," Marcus had warned, and Kyle had ignored the advice.

He glanced back. Her head was bowed over the grapes again. Her hands, usually so deft and sure were nervous, trembling. She wanted him—he knew that much. The way she responded to his touch was enough to make him crazy.

But she hadn't come to Maine for him, he reminded himself. She'd come for Victoria's advertising campaign and the men she hoped to meet during Race Week.

Men who would take her into their cabin, listen to her silken voice and magic laughter. Men who would kiss her and find her willing, eager, wanting them to love her—to fall in love with her.

Let them, he thought, turning away. Let them fall in love and marry her, the sooner the better. Then it would be over. He could leave for the sugar beaches of the Seychelles, knowing the magazine was in good hands with her as his new partner. But more importantly, knowing he wouldn't be tempted anymore.

Kyle picked up his wine and headed for the door. "I should think you'll be glad to see me gone once and for all. Then you can finally figure out what you really want."

Jeannie waited until he was gone, then leaned both hands on the counter and drew in a deep breath, letting it out slowly.

What in God's name had she been thinking about in coming here? If she couldn't be in a room full of people without wanting to touch him, to feel his mouth on hers, how did she expect to survive being alone with him in a cabin only fourteen feet long?

Yet none of it made sense. He liked antiques, she liked modern. He craved solitude while she needed people. But most importantly, he was a deeply sensuous man. Sex would be a vital part of life, while Jeannie had always thought of sex as pleasant, no big deal.

But if he was so wrong for her, why was she drawn to him this way? What perverse part of herself made her want to lead him on, understanding what it would be to give her love to a man like Kyle and welcoming the surrender even as the idea terrified her?

Even as she tried to convince herself that he was all wrong for her, Jeannie knew there was a side that was exactly right. A tender, caring and vulnerable side—one that dreamed as she did and was as confused as she was. The side that had opened her heart and made her want to slide into a love that could overpower and consume her. A love she wasn't even certain he would want if she offered it.

Jeannie made her way up the stairs, hesitating at the top as Kyle came toward her.

"It seems like I'm always apologizing," he said. "But I am sorry, Jeannie. I have a way of putting my foot into things when I'm with you. I just wish I could figure out why."

"Forget it," she said, trying for light and friendly, but only managing breathy and pathetic. So she opted for plain and simple instead. "Let's talk about the campaign for Victoria instead."

She watched him pull the folder out of his kit bag and set it on the table, his relief as evident as her own. "I thought an artist's concept of Victoria would be a good place to start. Side view only, with a large hat concealing her face."

While he sketched, Jeannie lay back on the bench, trying hard to concentrate.

Kyle watched her struggle, knowing this was as hard for her as it was for him, regardless of what she might tell herself.

And it would happen; he could feel it as surely as the change in the wind. Something this strong couldn't simply be willed away by either of them. The best he could hope for was that it would burn itself out by the time they had to leave.

10

Jeannie settled into the deep comfort of the old Adirondack chair and tucked her bare feet up under her. On one of the armrests sat two pairs of earrings: one of hammered gold, the other, soft black leather. Beside them sat a tall pilsner of icy cold beer, a local brand left in the fridge that morning by the infamous Dorothy.

In another hour, Kyle would be back to pick her up for her first Race Week party—a reception for sponsors and organizers at an exclusive yacht club—where she would spend the evening sipping champagne and turning down caviar with some of the East Coast's wealthiest families. But for now, she was content to simply relax and enjoy the rest of a pink-and-gold sunset from the comfort of Kyle's porch.

Sailboats, as graceful as swans, swept regally past her perch, heading into the harbor for the night while a lone gull screamed overhead—a straggler on his way home now that the day was over.

Jeannie wished him good-night, then lifted her glass and took a long swallow, finding it too bitter for her taste. Wiping the froth from her lip, she set the glass on the arm and picked up the earrings, laying the pairs side by side in the palm of her hand.

"Dress well," Kyle had advised her. "You'll need to impress the old money tonight."

So Jeannie had selected a frothy multicolored skirt that Lissa Stiller had given her, pairing it with a black cotton sweater that left her shoulders bare and dipped very low in the back. The perfect blend of "trash and class" Lissa had called it, and Jeannie hadn't had a clue when she would wear it, until that night.

Deciding to keep the effect simple, she'd gathered her hair into a simple ponytail, catching it with a gold-and-leather clip at the nape of her neck. Earrings would be her only other accessory, once she decided on a pair.

Untangling her legs, Jeannie stood up and snapped a gold earring into place. Tilting her head to the side, she studied her reflection in the window. The gold was good, but the leather might be better.

She was about to fasten one when the crunch of tires on gravel distracted her. Jeannie set the earrings on the armrest and walked to the edge of the porch. Kyle was early.

He looked up as he closed the door of the Land Rover and spotted her. Without thinking, Jeannie raised her hand and waved, feeling the unmistakable warmth of pleasure wash through her when he smiled—as though it was the most natural thing in the world for her to be standing there, waiting for him.

So she sat down instead.

"You're early," she called when he reached the stairs.

"I forgot to pack a jacket. I'm hoping there's one left in the closet upstairs."

But he didn't go into the house. Instead, he walked the length of the porch and sat on the arm of the chair next to her.

He motioned to the pilsner. "I see Dorothy has introduced you to our local brand. What do you think?"

Jeannie wrinkled her nose. "Not much."

"It's an acquired taste."

She grimaced as he took the glass and raised it to his lips. "I don't think a week will be long enough."

"Probably not," he agreed. "It usually takes a winter. One where the cold and fog lock in for days and nothing moves." He held the glass up. "When this is all there is, you learn to like it."

"And will you miss it when you go?"

Kyle grinned and placed the glass on the floor beside the chair. "Not at all. There are plenty of bad beers to be had around the world, believe me."

Jeannie followed his gaze to the gray, weathered shoreline. The sun was no more than a faint orange glow above the rocky cliffs now and the lights of the harbor shops were coming to life.

"I will miss the town though," he told her. "When I first came back, I didn't think I would ever fit in again—it had been so long. Now I can't imagine being anywhere else." Kyle looked over at her. "The reception will be starting soon. Are you ready?"

"Almost." She nodded at the earrings. "I just have to decide which of these to wear, and find my shoes. Then I'll be set."

"And here I figured you'd be all dressed and chomping at the bit to get over there."

"I meant to be, and then I came out to see the sunset and ended up staying longer than I intended. But it's almost over now."

She stood and walked to the railing. With every step, the gauzy skirt swirled around her legs, defining the shape of her thighs and the flare of her hips. The yacht club would never be the same, Kyle mused, already jealous of the men she'd dressed to please.

He watched the smooth, supple muscles of her back as she drew her shoulders up then pressed them down again.

He saw her wince as she pushed her shoulders back, and his jealousy was tempered with guilt. "What's wrong?"

"Nothing. I'm just a little sore."

Kyle rose and stood behind her, knowing he had worked her too hard that day. "It's bad right here, isn't it?" he said, running his hands lightly over her upper arms. "But here it's worse." He brushed a finger across her shoulder.

"How do you know?"

"Years of experience."

Her whole body stiffened as he took hold of her upper arms.

"What are you doing?"

Something I'll regret a minute from now, he thought. But to Jeannie he said, "Taking care of the pain." Gently his thumbs probed her aching muscles. "I won't do anything you don't want."

Her resistance gradually gave way as she arched her back and made a small, soft sound deep in her throat.

Kyle pressed his lips tightly together. Her skin was like satin, her scent the same heady floral he remembered from the gala. And holding her this way only made the wanting worse. But she was sore and it was his fault. The least he could do was try to give her some relief.

She sucked in a hissing breath when he found the knot and gradually kneaded it soft.

"Put your hands on the railing," he told her as he moved up to her shoulders.

"Why are you doing this?" she murmured as he worked his thumbs up and down the back of her neck.

"Because you won't be much good to me if you can't turn a winch tomorrow."

She smiled at him over her shoulder. "Very practical."

"Turn around," he growled, laying his palms on her neck and slowly stroking up to her nape, discovering she was soft and ticklish, then moving down across her shoulders and arms.

Her skin began to warm beneath his hands and he felt the precise moment when her breathing changed. Instinctively, his touch lightened, becoming a caress. For Kyle, the massage was no longer therapeutic. Now it was the first slow dance of seduction.

Bending close, he touched his lips to one graceful shoulder, then grazed a moist, tender path to her neck.

Jeannie tilted her head to the side, lost in the sweet sensations and suddenly very aware of the brush of the earring against her neck, the scent of her own perfume and the tingling in the tips of her breasts.

The urge to move was almost unbearable. To feel the rub of lace against her nipples, slightly rough, just like his hand; to squeeze her thighs together in answer to the pulse that beat there, faint but insistent.

"The reception will be starting soon," he said, his voice low and husky in her ear. "We should be going."

"But I'm not ready," she breathed. "I haven't decided on the earrings yet."

"Let me help." He unclipped the earring and put it in his shirt pocket.

"No earrings?" she murmured, shivering as he nipped at her earlobe.

"You don't need them. You don't need anything."

Jeannie heard the faint snick of the hair clip; then his hands were in her hair, shaking it loose and spreading it across her shoulders.

"Why did you do that?"

"So I can do this." Pressing her forward, he swept her hair up and kissed the nape of her neck.

There was no lethargy now, only the pounding of her heart and the heat of his mouth as he turned her to face him.

"Jeannie," he whispered. But she only shook her head.

She didn't want to think, or talk or listen to the sane voices inside her mind telling her to stop him, to stop herself.

She hadn't come to Maine for Victoria. She knew that now. She'd come for herself. This was exactly where she wanted to be, and he was the man she wanted to be with.

He spoke her name again and Jeannie leaned into him, closing her eyes and letting the heat build as he smoothed his palms over her back and lowered his mouth to hers. His tongue was like velvet as it dipped between her lips, tasting her with the maddening care she knew so well. Ever so slowly, he took her down, drowning any lingering protest as he stoked the fire that had smoldered too long between them.

Jeannie opened more to him, her mouth greedy, taking what he gave and demanding more, lost in the feel and the taste and the smell of him; wanting to be thoroughly explored and filled and give nothing in return. His grip tightened, fastening her against him and she met his fire with her own.

She tugged at his tie, fumbled with his buttons, needing to feel his skin, his heat, to know he burned as she did and wanting him to quench the flames that already crackled and danced deep inside.

He lifted her sweater up and off, and she clung to him, rubbing her breasts across his naked chest and damning the thin layer of lace that constrained her. Then it, too, was gone and there was no turning back.

There was only here and now, and the lure of his mouth and the promise of passion in his hands as he swept her up and rocked her hard against him.

Nothing existed but the two of them, there on a point of rock where the waves crashed forever and the distant lights of the harbor twinkled like a fairyland as his mouth roamed over her throat and her breasts. He took each waiting nipple in turn, sucking and nipping until Jeannie sagged beneath him, her bones surely melting. When he scooped her up in his arms, carrying her to the door and up the stairs, she buried her face in his shoulder, knowing none of it was real. None of it would last. Only hoping it would be enough.

Twilight shadows filled the room, stealing the colors and leaving behind only black and white images. Dark mahogany, stark white sheets and a duvet that now seemed as deep and cool as the ocean below them. Jeannie closed her eyes as Kyle eased her down to his bed, tumbling the neat line of pillows all around her.

Dorothy's lilacs, the blooms now fully opened and heavy with nectar, drooped lazily over the crystal vase, their perfume filling Jeannie's head as the bed dipped beneath Kyle's weight.

He knelt over her, his thighs straddling her waist, his arms locked on either side. "Look at me," he ordered.

Jeannie opened her eyes. Even in shadow, she could see the harsh, dark hunger glittering in his eyes, hear it in each ragged breath. Gone was all semblance of civility. The suits, the ties, the carefully pressed collars. Here was only the man, strong and powerful above her, his need as raw, as naked as her own.

Trembling as much with joy as with fear, Jeannie reached up with both hands, curving her fingers around the face she'd longed to explore for so long, stroking her thumbs across the lips that could bring her so much pleasure; marveling that such passion and desire could exist between two people.

"Tell me what you want," he whispered.

"You." She circled his neck, tried to pull him down. "I want you."

"Where?" he demanded, arms locked and unmoving as he gazed into her eyes.

Everywhere, Jeannie thought, but turned her head away, not certain she could answer.

He tipped her face back and bent to touch his lips to hers, suddenly gentle again. "Here?" He all but stopped her breath when he drew her lower lip between his teeth, then moved lower until his mouth was at her breasts. "And here?" he asked, his breath teasing her nipples until she arched off the bed, certain she would scream if he didn't touch her.

"Yes," she breathed, hearing him chuckle softly as she guided him to her aching, swollen breasts.

"Then tell me." His tongue skimmed over her skin. "I need to know you want this as much as I do. I need to hear you say it."

"I want this. I want you...everywhere," she told him, and he took one breast into his mouth, sucking and sucking as the heat inside her spread out in ever-widening circles. "My mouth," she gasped. "My breasts..."

"Go on," he said as he slid down farther, pressing openmouthed kisses across the soft plain of her belly, stopping at the waistband of her skirt. He lifted his head. "Where else?"

In a quick bold move that shocked her, Jeannie showed him.

Kyle's fingers stroked her through the lace. "Now I understand."

He watched her shudder as he tugged the skirt down. Heard her say his name, no more than a breathless sigh, when the lace was taken away. Her legs parted at his slightest touch, and it was all he could do keep from taking her then, hard and fast, as every impulse in his body urged him to do.

But he held back, wanting it to last. Wanting to find

what pleased her most and take her to the edge again and again, until she was limp with longing and there was nothing in her restless mind but him.

"Do you know how long I've wanted to see you like this?" he whispered, knowing she wasn't yet accustomed to his blunt way but determined she would learn. "How often I've dreamed of touching you this way. To feel you rise against my hand, yes, just like that."

Open and vulnerable as she'd never been before, Jeannie clutched at the duvet as his lips touched the sensitive flesh of her inner thighs. She drove her fingers into his hair, seeking more and more as she gave herself over completely to him. And all the while, his voice, hypnotic and dangerous, wove around her, pinning her to his bed as he slowly drove her mad.

Shameless now, Jeannie begged, writhing and bucking as he murmured encouragement. Never had she felt so wild, so reckless. And never had she lain so helpless in a man's arms when release finally came.

Kyle waited as long as he could then pulled away, cursing as he tugged at his belt, his own need made desperate by the depth of her response. But then Jeannie's fingers were there, closing over the buckle and holding him spellbound as she slowly threaded leather through metal.

Pale moonlight had crept into the room through the open shutters, bathing her skin with its soft glow. Like porcelain she was, fine and delicate, until he looked into her eyes. Fire, hot and fierce, the source of her strength, and the part of her he craved as much as the surrender.

"Do you know how long I've wanted to do this?" she asked, a smile curving her lips as she stripped away the last of his clothes. "And this?"

Never had a woman's touch burned him so completely. He shuddered with each frank and beautiful movement, gritting his teeth and dangerously close to losing even the fragile thread of control he had left.

She led them now, taking him down, feeling her power.

"Do you know what I want?" she murmured, taking him with her as she lay back on the nest of pillows.

"Tell me," Kyle groaned as he settled between her thighs and buried his face in the heated perfume of her throat.

Her teeth grazed his ear as she whispered the words he longed to hear, and the thread broke. Rising over her, he pushed himself into the center of her soul, knowing he wouldn't last long and needing to fill her completely.

And Jeannie took him, wrapping herself around him, becoming part of him with each powerful thrust. Holding him close as every muscle in his body tensed and he rose above her, shouting her name in triumph. Feeling that same triumph within herself as he collapsed on her, spent and sated. And hers.

They lay together for a long time, legs and arms twined, listening to each other breathe, feeling each other's pulse gradually calm and return to normal. When at last she shivered with cold, he pulled the duvet over them, wrapping them both in the lingering heat and scent of their lovemaking.

He propped himself up on one elbow. "I have to tell you something."

Jeannie opened one eye. "Is it time for confessions already?"

"Must be."

She dragged her foot up his leg, enjoying the feel of crisp, coarse hair against her toes. "Okay, go."

"I lied when I told you I came early to find a jacket. I purposely left it behind, knowing there were none here and I wouldn't get into the reception without one."

Jeannie sat up. "But why?"

"Because I knew if we went, I couldn't go in with you. I couldn't sit back and watch you smile at other men and want you this much for myself."

"So you planned this?"

"In a way I suppose I did. But I didn't have time for candles and a fire."

"I forgive you."

Laughing, he drew her down beside him, his fingertips tracing a long, sweet line up and down her body. "Are you happy, then?"

"Very." She sighed and let her eyes close.

"Then promise me something. Promise you'll only wear this perfume from now on."

She looked into his eyes, not understanding.

So he brushed his lips across the places where he knew she applied her perfume: the hollow at the base of her throat, the sensitive spots behind each ear and finally her wrists, feeling her pulse begin to race. "I don't want to guess anymore," he explained. "I want to know that this one particular scent is you. And when you wear it, you're remembering the first time we made love. Just as I will be."

"The first time?" she teased. "What makes you think there'll be a second?"

"This," he growled, his hand already busy, slowly taking her up to a height she hadn't dreamed possible.

Later, when the second storm passed, she slept in his arms, protected, coddled and completely satisfied, both of them curled on the right side of his bed.

It was after midnight when she felt him stir, trying in vain to leave without waking her.

"Sorry," he mumbled, pressing a quick kiss on the top of her head as he fastened his belt. "But I'm starving.

Do you want to come down or shall I bring you up something?''

"I'll come down." She swung her legs over the side and stared at her crumpled skirt. "But I don't think I'll wear that again."

Going to his closet, Kyle pulled out her robe and held it open for her. "I like having your clothes in there. But mostly I like having them off of you."

"Rude." She laughed, slapping at his hands when he refused to let her close the robe.

"Get used to it." Taking her hand, he led her out to the stairs.

Jeannie followed him into the kitchen, wondering what he meant and afraid to hope. Did he mean for now, or for always? Or just until he left?

He leaned into the fridge. "How's tortellini and Caesar salad sound?"

Jeannie came up from behind and wrapped her arms around him, pushing aside everything but the moment. "Sounds wonderful."

He turned in the circle of her embrace and gazed down at her, studying her, as though trying to find a way into her mind.

"I don't know what's happening here, either," he said at last. "I just know I don't want it to end." His mouth fastened on hers, his kiss fast and deep this time, almost knocking her off balance.

Holding on to his arms, she smoothed her tongue over his, feeling his grip tighten as she dipped inside his mouth to do some sampling of her own. Then she dragged her lips away and watched him draw in a long, unsteady breath.

"If you don't stop," he warned, "we won't eat for another hour."

When the pasta was eaten and the salad bowl scraped

dry, Jeannie leaned back with her glass of wine. "That was marvelous. Thank you."

Kyle loaded the last of the silver into the dishwasher then sat down and raised his glass in a toast. "To the first meal we've eaten in peace."

"I was thinking the same thing," she said, laughing as she touched her glass to his. "Maybe the trick is to skip lunch."

"Or to make love more often."

Jeannie held up a hand. "Can we just talk for a few minutes?"

"Okay." He sipped at his wine. "What shall we talk about? For a few minutes."

Jeannie propped her chin on her fists. "You."

"I'm pretty dull stuff."

"Let me be the judge. After all, you know a lot about me, but I know so little about you."

"You know what's important."

"But I want to know more."

He shrugged. "Like what?"

She settled back. "For starters, I want to know what you meant when you said you've lived most of your life alone."

"Exactly that."

Jeannie heard the warning in his tone, but wasn't about to give up. "Tell me why. I know your mother died when you were little, but what about your father?"

Kyle hesitated, obviously considering, then leaned forward, resting his arms on the table. "My father was a shipbuilder here in Bristol Harbor. One of the best on the coast."

He paused, turning the glass slowly between his hands. "From what I understand, some of his boats are still in operation, and I'm not surprised. He was a real craftsman.

I can still see him, tramping through the woodlot in huge leather boots, searching for the perfect mast.''

Jeannie watched him smile at his private memories, and instinctively reached out to cover his hand with hers. ''Sounds like you were very close.''

Kyle linked his fingers with hers, his thumb stroking across hers as his smile faded. ''We might have been. He was killed in a sailing accident when I was fifteen.''

''Oh, Kyle.''

''It was the damnedest thing about him. Lived all his life by the sea but never learned to swim.''

''And what happened to you?''

''I went to live with his brother in Chicago. An attorney. Single, successful, lived in a fancy condo. He gave me a room, told me to call him Ted, then left me pretty much alone.''

''How could he do that?''

Kyle looked at her. ''You misunderstand. Ted was a good man. It must have been difficult for him to suddenly be saddled with a teenager. Especially one who skipped school and hung around the harbor all day.''

He brushed a stray lock of hair from his face and Jeannie could imagine him as that teenager, sitting alone on the docks, and her own heart ached for him. ''You must have missed your dad and Bristol Harbor very much.''

Kyle turned away. ''I never admitted it to anyone. And after a while, I got to like where I was. Eventually Chicago became part of me. Ted's life-style rubbed off and became something I wanted, too. Later it was Duncan's life-style I wanted. The only part of my father that remained was the sailing. Every summer, I crewed with the charters and eventually bought my own boat.''

''And Bristol Harbor?''

Capturing her hand again, Kyle pressed his lips to her fingertips. ''It was years before I came back. I was on business in Bangor, and just kept driving. I saw the house we lived in, the woodlot, the barn where my dad built the boats. Everything.''

She waited for him to continue, watching his hands on hers, holding her as though somehow afraid she would escape; wishing she had the courage to tell him she had nowhere to run.

"I ran into a man who had worked with my dad. We sat on his porch drinking beer and remembering. Eventually he brought out a box he said he'd been holding for years. In it was a set of drawings for a boat the two of them had dreamed of building. The perfect ocean vessel for a single-hander.''

"The boat you've built," Jeannie said, her voice soft with the wonder of what Kyle had done.

His smile was as warm and welcome as sunshine in February. "That's right. In the same box were detailed plans for the voyage my father planned to take in that boat—a three-year solo around the world. But he never had the chance." Kyle released her hand and sat back. "So I decided to make it for him. And that's why I'm here. To fulfill his dream.''

"A dream that will take you away from the one place you love." Jeannie lowered her eyes. "And away from me.''

"Yes.''

A simple, honest answer. Nothing less than she'd expect.

The chair scraped across the wooden floor as he rose and held out a hand. "Now come back to bed."

11

It was almost noon when Kyle climbed the stairs again. He and Jeannie had finally fallen asleep as the sky was beginning to lighten, her head a comforting weight on his shoulder. But he'd been up again only a few hours later, already adjusting to the limited sleep pattern he would have to maintain at sea.

Normally, he would have gone straight to the boat. But for the first time in years, there had been someone else to consider. So he'd spent the morning working, reading and waiting. Finding the house oddly quiet and lifting his head at every sound. Listening for her footsteps on the stairs, her voice in the hall. Wanting to see her smile and hear her laugh. Then kiss her lips and know she was still there for him. Strange longings, for a man who'd never needed anything he couldn't provide for himself.

He opened the door and surveyed the room. Lilacs overturned, sheets in a twist and candles everywhere. And in the middle of it all, Jeannie. Hair like a flame against the battered linen, hands curled innocently by her cheek—sound asleep. Completely oblivious to the sun streaming in the window, the gulls screaming in the distance. And him.

He blew out a long breath, remembering the way that hair had skimmed his chest when she bent over him. The way those nails had raked his skin as she kissed his throat, his belly, his thighs. And hearing again her sweet, low moan as she took him into her mouth, making him feel wanted in a way no other woman ever had. And probably never would again.

Her eyes opened when he sat on the edge of the bed, and for one fleeting moment, Kyle hesitated, unsure how he would react if he saw regret in those eyes. Or worse, indifference.

She blinked twice, focused. And then she smiled—a slow, lazy curve of the lips that had him smiling back.

"What are you doing out there?" she whispered and lifted the covers. "Get back in here."

He stretched out next to her, pulling her close, loving the feel of her warm, naked body against his fully clothed one; knowing with sudden clarity that this thing with Jeannie Renamo was not going to burn itself out quickly.

Her mouth opened at the first touch of his lips, accepting his kiss fully, naturally—as though it was his right.

"I guess we'll be a little late for the sailing trial," she murmured as she pushed the shirt from his shoulders.

"A little."

"But what about Matt and Jack?"

"I'm not sharing," he said as he moved over her.

When again he lay beside her, his hair damp with sweat and his breathing still heavy, Jeannie propped herself up on her elbows and gazed down at him. His eyes drifted open and he reached up to smooth back her hair. She couldn't remember when she'd last been so content just to be with a man.

"Is it time to get up?" she asked, nipping the end of his nose.

"It's way past time." He locked his arm around her neck and dragged her down, kissing her solidly. Then he sat up and put his legs over the side. She watched him put on his jeans, thinking what a shame it was to cover such legs, to say nothing of the rest of him.

He held out a hand. "Come on. I told Matt we'd sail down to Davisport sometime today."

Reluctantly she let him pull her to her feet. "Was he upset that you canceled the trial?"

Kyle's hands rested on her hips, casual, possessive. "To be honest, he was glad to sleep in. He and his wife run a pub down there and it keeps them up pretty late. But he's looking forward to meeting the fourth crew member." He checked the clock on the nightstand. "Although he's probably given up on us by now."

"Then I'd better get ready." She toppled him back on the bed and headed for the door. On impulse, she nabbed her bottle of perfume as she passed the dresser. "I'm going to have a bath." She glanced back at him, the bottle dangling from her fingers. "Will you join me? Or shall I lock you out again?"

"Don't even try."

Eyes closed, Jeannie leaned back and inhaled the decidedly male scent of his soap as he rubbed it over her body. Enjoying the way it blended with her perfume to create something completely new and different. And totally unexpected.

Bath finished, he rose from the water and wrapped her in one of his towels then grabbed one for himself and fastened it at his waist. She watched in the mirror as he drew the towel over her body, drying all the places he had touched her, kissed her, loved her.

She saw her nipples rise, hard and pouting as his hands circled her breasts; heard her breath catch as he moved lower, cupping her sex but not quite touching, just letting the warmth of his hand surround her. She felt her legs open for him and watched his eyes darken as she lifted her hips, letting them both know she was his for the taking.

His eyes held hers in the mirror, defying her to look away as he stroked her. But she wouldn't. She knew by now that love with Kyle could never be timid or shy. Not if it was to survive. And she did love him; there was no question in her mind anymore.

Loved his honesty, his passion and the very strength that had always frightened her, because it was part of him—part of her now. And she wouldn't change it even if she could.

He could be ruthless, yes. But he was also a man of dreams and wonder. A man capable of real tenderness and compassion.

She knew he would take care of her if she let him, protect her even if she wouldn't. But did he love her? Would he even want to know that she loved him? And when September came, would he miss her at all?

Making up her mind she wasn't going to look for answers, Jeannie took hold of his hands. "Stop," she said, smiling at his confused expression. Lifting his fingertips to her lips, she softly kissed each one. "Not for ever, just for now. The next time we make love, I want it to be in the boat." She touched her mouth to his. "But I want to meet your friends first."

A few hours later, Jeannie stepped over the top rail of the boat and onto the dock to help Kyle with the moorings. "Davisport certainly is different from Bristol Harbor," she called as she knelt to secure the knot. "So quiet."

"For now." Kyle tested the moorings then took her hand. "Give it another couple of weeks and it'll be just as busy as every other summer town. Bristol Harbor simply gets a jump on the season by holding the race early."

He linked his fingers with hers as they started up the dock.

"So how did I do today?" Jeannie asked.

"Fine. What you lack in experience, you make up for in sheer determination." He stopped at the end of the dock. "You're a formidable crew member, Jeannie. I'm lucky to have you. Here and at *Aspects.*"

Aspects. Jeannie stared ahead as they continued up the hill into town. This was the first time he'd mentioned the magazine since yesterday.

They'd talked about everything else. Lying together in the dark, making confessions, comparing notes. She'd told him about Marcus, he'd told her about Magda. They'd covered colleges, books, movies—as though they needed to fill in the blanks as quickly as possible before it was too late. But never once had they spoken of *Aspects,* or Victoria. And for now, Jeannie was content to have it stay that way.

"What's the name of Matt's pub again?" she asked as they strolled by the windows on Davisport's main street.

"The Fo'c'sle." He pointed ahead. "Up there on the left. It's popular in the summer, but shouldn't be too crowded this time of year."

Which was why he wasn't ready for the scene that greeted them when he opened the door. The music was loud, the air heavy with smoke and the room packed with sunburned men and women of all ages.

"This is great," Jeannie shouted above the din. "I had no idea it would be like this."

"Neither did I," he muttered, wondering if it was too late to change his mind.

The music ended just as a hostess with the name Sandy embroidered on her white T-shirt greeted them. "Come on in, though I have to warn you, it's sharing room only."

"What's going on anyway?" Kyle asked.

She handed him a leaflet. "Our own Battle of the Bands. Been going on all afternoon. The next one up will be…" She ran a finger down the list. "Gilded Cage. Can I get you some seats?"

Kyle was about to refuse when a voice hailed him from the bar. Across the sea of faces, a huge bear of a man raised one arm and waved. Matt, Kyle realized, and felt himself smile.

To Matt's right, his tiny bird of a wife, Vicky, finished pulling a pitcher of beer, then blew Kyle a two-handed kiss.

Matt called in one of the waitresses to take over the bar and then was on his way, weaving through the crowd with Vicky in tow. It never failed to surprise Kyle that a man of Matt's size could move with such speed and grace. But it was exactly that combination of strength and agility that made him an invaluable member of the racing team.

"You made it," Matt roared, passing up Kyle's hand in favor of a bone-crushing hug.

"I told you we would."

"And just in time, too," Vicky said, pushing her husband aside and jumping up to wrap her arms around Kyle's neck. "Gilded Cage is about to start." Her green eyes all but disappeared behind a wide grin. "Just the kind of music you love."

"Don't worry," Matt told him. "Three songs and they're off. Even you can take that." He clapped an arm around Kyle's shoulder and turned to Jeannie. "You must be the reason Kyle canceled out on us today." He held out a hand. "Name's Matt."

"Jeannie Renamo. Nice to meet you."

Vicky elbowed her way past him. "And I'm Vicky. The wife." Laughing, Jeannie took her hand, thinking what a study in opposites Kyle's friends were. One so big and dark, the other so tiny and fair. But somehow they fit together perfectly.

"So where's this crewman we're all dying to meet?" Matt demanded.

"You're looking at her," Kyle told him.

"A woman?" Matt started to laugh. "Well, this is a first. And I for one am glad of it. You've done a lot of racing, then, have you, Jeannie?"

"Actually, none at all." She paused, watching his reaction.

Matt struggled for a moment, then the smile returned. "In that case, you've come to the right place. I'll get us a pitcher of beer and we can tell you all about the intricacies of racing with Kyle Hunter."

"I'd like that," Jeannie said, looking over at Kyle. "Because I've still got a hell of a lot to learn."

"It's settled, then," Matt said. "Come and sit."

Jeannie saw Kyle eye the stage, hesitating. Vicky skirted around him to where Jeannie stood. "You come and he'll follow," she whispered. "I guarantee it."

Jeannie held up her hands in a gesture of helplessness and let herself be led, watching Kyle's expression of disbelief turn to one of resigned amusement.

"Told you he'd follow," Vicky said as Jeannie sat down. "I can tell that look on the man's face a mile off."

Jeannie was tempted to ask Vicky what it was she saw. To find out if she'd ever seen it there before and to know what had happened after. But instead she asked, "Have you and Matt known Kyle long?"

"Forever. We all went to school together." She pointed to the bar. "I'll go get that pitcher."

Kyle and Matt sat down just as Vicky reappeared with the beer and four glasses. They bantered easily back and forth while Vicky poured, and Jeannie felt an odd twinge of jealousy as she watched them.

Matt and Vicky were part of this world, the one Kyle was anxious to return to. While she was part of that other world in Chicago. The one he could hardly wait to leave.

A manic three-chord intro effectively put an end to any more conversation. Jeannie watched Kyle's head snap around, saw his eyes narrow at the three young women on stage.

"He won't last an hour," Vicky said, laughing.

"Sure he will," Jeannie argued. "He's more tolerant than that."

Vicky turned her head slowly. "You think so?"

Jeannie recognized that look, that tone. She picked up her beer and sat back. "Definitely. And five bucks says I'm right."

Behind them, the lead singer growled and strutted, shouted and stomped, punctuating her words with the jab of a long red fingernail at the crowd on the dance floor.

Vicky smiled. "One hour. Five bucks." Leaning over, she punched her husband on the arm. "Come on. We've got work to do." She stood and grinned at Kyle. "Enjoy the band," she said, then winked at Jeannie as she slid across the seat. "I like you, Jeannie Renamo. I hope you'll be around for a while."

Jeannie nodded. "Me, too."

A shattering guitar riff marked the end of the first number. Kyle moved around to Jeannie's side of the table, mumbling something about "two more" as he dragged his beer over.

Jeannie smiled at him. "You don't come to places like this often, do you?"

"Not if I can help it." He glanced over his shoulder at the band. "Maybe if I could understand the words it would make a difference."

"Don't try so hard. You have to let the music float over you. And the best place to do that is on the dance floor. Come on."

She tried to nudge him along the bench but Kyle sat firm. "I don't dance."

"Everyone dances." She ducked under the table and came up on the other side. "It's only natural."

Kyle couldn't believe he was letting himself be led to the square of hardwood in front of the band. Once there, he wanted to keep to the edge, well out of the crush of swaying bodies.

But Jeannie kept going, squeezing her way into the heart of the crowd, right where she would always be. And oddly, he didn't want to be anywhere else but beside her.

She took his face in her hands, bringing it close to hers. "Don't try to make sense of it," she yelled, laughing. "Just dance."

Kyle tried to match her movements, but only succeeded in making her laugh even harder. "Relax," she told him.

"I am," he muttered. Then he looked at her and started to laugh. And gradually the movements became easier and the music less grating. The next song was about lost love and vampire bats as far as he could tell, but the lyrics had ceased to matter a while ago. About the same time he realized he was having fun.

He knew that Jeannie was changing him, subtly, in ways he couldn't even name. Filling an emptiness that had been part of him for so long, he'd forgotten it was there. And the idea of leaving her filled him with dread.

The music changed again, slowing and smoothing, becoming almost melodic. Kyle brought her in close, tucking her head under his chin and settling his arms around her. The scent of the sea was in her hair, on her skin, mingling with the perfume she wore for him and making him wish he'd met her sooner, or later. Or maybe not at all.

They swayed to the music, barely moving as one song flowed into the next, their bodies touching intimately while he traced a slow line up and down her spine.

Strong fingers curved around the nape of her neck and tilted her back, angling her to receive him. Then he held her there, his eyes dark and intense again, searching her face as though he would find the answer to some question if he only looked long enough.

She longed to tell him it was all right. He could ask her anything and she would answer. Do you love me? And she would say yes. And will you wait? And the answer would be yes. Forever.

But the words were new and strange to her and so refused to come, leaving her breathless and frustrated by her own cowardice.

The music stopped and the sudden silence was abrupt, offensive.

Kyle took her by the hand. "Let's go."

She asked him to wait by the door. There was something she had forgotten.

Vicky was at the cash register, punching in drink orders. She looked up when Jeannie slipped a five-dollar bill into the till. "You lost, huh?"

"No," Jeannie said, smiling. "I won."

In a cove just north of Davisport, they doused the sails and dropped anchor, doing only what was absolutely necessary to secure the boat before racing each other to the privacy of the cabin.

Jeannie hadn't even reached the bottom step before Kyle's hands were on her, turning her around and dragging her hard against him. He spoke her name, no more than a harsh whisper against her lips, then covered her mouth with his, and they were both spinning, caught in the heart of the storm that raged between them.

Impatient now, they clawed at buttons, tore at zippers, all the while their mouths clinging, keeping the contact that suddenly seemed vital to both.

He kicked open the door of his cabin and was not gentle as he lay her back on his bed. She hadn't truly appreciated how strong he was until that moment and she knew a brief moment of fear. Felt it as a tiny shudder deep inside when he loomed over her, his hair falling in his eyes, his eyes burning into hers, his breath hot on her skin.

He must have sensed it, because he touched her face, his fingertips trembling. "Are you afraid of me?"

She saw the flicker of vulnerability, the uncertainty and wondered how she could have ever feared this tender, gentle man.

Taking his face in her hands, she drew him down. "No. Not anymore."

"I hope not. Because I need you, Jeannie." He moved over her, stroking her hair as he kissed her lips. "And I haven't needed anybody for so long, I don't think I could stand it if you shut me out now."

She let her knees fall open wide and rose to meet him. "I could never shut you out, Kyle. Never."

There was no preamble this time, no whispered words. Only a need to be deep inside her. To feel her close around him. To make her his.

He felt her open more as he moved within her, her body molding itself to him, taking his shape. He slid his hands under her, lifting her higher as he thrust into her, farther, deeper; holding himself still as the first wave rippled through her and into him.

Then he was moving again, slowly, while she calmed and found the rhythm. And then faster and harder, pour-

ing himself into her while she cried his name again and
again.

Jeannie sat at the kitchen table the next morning, rubbing her eyes and not regretting for a minute the lack of
sleep.

But she passed on the cream and sipped her coffee
black, hoping it would wake her up quicker. "What time
are we meeting Matt and Vicky?"

Kyle concentrated on flipping the eggs. "Nine
o'clock." He looked up as the phone started to ring.
"Unless that's him now with a change of plans. Do you
want to get it?"

"Sure." Jeannie dragged herself out of the chair and
dashed down the hall into his office. The caller turned
out to be Dorothy, and her tone turned jubilant when
Jeannie answered.

"Just tell him I'll be round shortly to do the cleaning
up. Don't you two worry about a thing."

Jeannie smiled as she hung up the phone. "It was Dorothy. She's coming by shortly."

"I'll lay you odds she's here before we've finished.
Just to get a look at you."

"I hope she's not too disappointed." Jeannie called as
she crossed to the fax machine in the corner. "You've
got a fax here."

She looked up to find Kyle standing in the doorway.
"I'll take it."

Jeannie held the page out. "Of course."

Kyle read it over quickly, then looked up at her. "We
should talk."

Jeannie felt herself stiffen and tried to relax. "About
what?"

"I sent a note to the printer's this morning canceling

the Boulderbottom column." He laid the fax on his desk. "This is the confirmation that they were able to do it."

Jeannie stared at the paper then at Kyle, trying to make sense of what he was saying. Trying to reconcile the concern in his eyes with the cruelty of his words. But there was no way to do it. And still he kept talking.

"I couldn't think of any other way to handle it."

Anger, betrayal. It all rushed at her at once. She wrapped her arms around herself and backed away. "How could you do this to me again? How could you cancel Victoria and not say a word to me first?"

He came slowly toward her. "Come on, Jeannie. What did you expect? Did you think we could go back to Chicago and pretend nothing happened? That you could just pick up where you left off as Victoria Boulderbottom?"

She kept moving backward, staying just out of reach. "I didn't know what to expect. I tried not to think about it."

He took hold of her arms, making her stand still. "Well, think about it now. I won't let you start into it again, Jeannie. I can't. Not when I need you so badly myself."

"What are you suggesting?"

His hands were warm, compelling, as he slipped them around her waist. "That we spend as much time together as possible before I have to leave. That we go back to Chicago at the end of the week and start winning those Pulitzers for you." He slid his fingers into her hair and drew her closer. "I can't promise you anything, Jeannie, but I can offer you this. Let me create a new position for you. Help me turn *Aspects* into the kind of magazine you'd like to work for. The kind I've always wanted it to be."

She shoved him back. "This is the consolation prize then, is it? A nice parting gift for our guest?"

"You misunderstand me."

"Do I, Kyle? Then help me out here. You canceled my column this morning, while it's at a peak, without a word to me, because you need me. Because you want to be with me."

"Yes."

"But only until September. Then you'll be fine again, is that it?"

She could see the anger rising in him now. "You're twisting my words."

"Tell me where I've got it wrong, then. Tell me you didn't just offer me a big promotion, the chance for a dream, in return for sex from now until September. Tell me I heard all that wrong. Because right now, Kyle, that's all I see."

"I didn't mean it like that. I care about you, Jeannie. I just can't offer you more."

"I didn't ask for a damn thing."

"I know that."

"Then how dare you insult me like this." She turned and walked from the den on feet that were already numb.

He reached her at the bottom of the stairs. "Jeannie, please, I want you to understand."

She paused with her hand on the railing but wouldn't look at him. "I do understand. What you really want is to make me convenient. Easy to dismiss when the time comes." She turned to him slowly. "But I won't let you. So you can fax them now and tell them to continue to run 'Marrying Well' because I'm going to finish my series. And it isn't about love anymore, Kyle. Now it's only about winning."

12

Jeannie grabbed the phone on the fifth ring, jamming the receiver between her ear and shoulder while she continued to type. "I know, I know, the column's late. It'll be ready by noon. I promise."

"Sure. Just like you promised to call and tell me how things have been going out there in Montana all these weeks."

Jeannie lifted her hands from the keyboard. "Magda?" Holding the receiver in one hand now, Jeannie rubbed the back of her neck with the other. "How are you?"

"Lousy. Desmond's still in England and no one around here appreciates a bear claw like you do." Jeannie heard the rustle of wax paper and smiled, the tension already starting to drain.

"Anyway," Magda continued, "I didn't call to talk about me. I've got a meeting coming up with the new publisher, then I'm off to New York for a few days. But I had to know how you're doing. And Stuart, too, of course."

"We're fine," Jeannie told her, then rose and carried the phone to the window. Stuart was standing by the paddock, talking to a group of men. As though sensing her there, Stuart looked up, his smile as genuine, his pleasure as real as the day she'd arrived. Guilt tweaked her heart as she smiled and waved, wishing she could be honest with him, let him know what she was really doing there, but knowing the timing was wrong.

"Just fine," she repeated. "Stuart's getting ready for Alaska, of course. And me, well you know what I'm doing."

"Winning big, it looks like. Victoria hit the local talk shows this morning. Every station has someone with a Boulderbottom poster asking the same question, 'Are Women Who Marry For Money Really Happy?'"

"That's great," Jeannie said, but didn't bother to ask what the conclusions had been. She wandered back to the desk and sat down. "And what are you up to these days?"

"Not much...oh damn, Trish's out in the hall flapping her hands at me. Which means she's either drying her nails or I'm late for the meeting. I'll call next week." Magda hesitated a moment. "So you're really all right, then?"

Jeannie kept a smile in her voice. "Couldn't be better."

Magda's voice softened. "I hope so."

Jeannie held on long after Magda was gone, only hanging up when she heard Stuart's boots in the hall outside her office.

Her office. That was how he termed it. Really, it was his library. A wonderful room of windows and sunlight, filled with books and comfortable chairs. She'd spent so much time there during the rehab benefit weekend that Stuart had assumed it was where she was most comfortable.

In truth, she'd merely been hiding—from his guests, his illustrious speakers and him, feigning headaches and heat exhaustion in the hopes of being left alone. She should have given the assignment to someone who could cover the event properly. But Kyle had just returned from Race Week and she'd had nowhere else to go.

She suspected now that Stuart had known all along what she was doing, but had said nothing. He'd simply brought her a glass of wine from time to time, or a plate of food from the buffet. And every night he'd escorted her to her room, telling her again how glad he was that she'd come.

She'd started to feel so comfortable, that when he'd asked her to stay on and do an exclusive on The Big River Foundation, she'd said yes immediately, welcoming the refuge he offered.

So he'd set up a computer and she'd set to work: learning about his causes, his life-style, even how to sit a horse. All the while keeping her Boulderbottom column a secret, and sending the weekly instalments to Trish by modem.

Stuart knocked on the door, then opened it. Jeannie reached out and darkened the screen, covering up the evidence once again.

"Working hard?" he asked.

She smiled. "I'm past deadline. Again."

"You'll make it. You always do." He rested his hands on her shoulders. "I only hope you'll let me read your work one day." He sounded almost wistful and Jeannie knew she couldn't keep the column and Victoria from him much longer.

"You're tense," he said, testing her muscles with his fingertips. "I can fix that."

Jeannie bent her head forward as he worked his fingers up her neck. His touch was soothing and gentle. But instead of relaxing, all she could think of was the night on Kyle's porch, and a touch that could turn her to liquid.

She put her hands over his. "Thanks. That's great."

Stuart swiveled the chair around and lifted her to her feet. "Glad to help."

Framing her face with his hands, he lowered his perfect mouth to hers. His kiss was like a warm breeze, carrying her somewhere safe, somewhere far from the storm of Kyle's passion. But leaving her oddly sad.

"Stuart," she whispered, pulling away as gently as she could.

He ran a hand over his face, pushed it through his hair. "I understand." He motioned to the love seat. "Will you sit a moment? I want to talk to you." He sank down next to her. "I'll make this simple. I want you to come with me to Alaska."

"I don't—"

"Hear me out. I believe we can be good together, Jeannie. My work takes me to all the troubled places in the world and your work lets you record what you see there. With your ability, you could make a real difference to the people who need it most."

She leaned back. "I admit the idea is intriguing, but I'll have to see if the magazine will fund me."

"They won't need to."

"Absolutely not. You cannot pay my expenses. I won't allow— "

"Jeannie," he cut in. "I'm trying to ask you to marry me. I want you to go as my wife."

For the first time in years, Jeannie had nothing to say, even though a simple yes would do it. Victoria could go out on a blaze of glory, she'd win the bet and life would start over in Alaska with a man who cared for her, respected her work and wanted to be with her. But what finally came out was "Stuart, I have something to tell you."

He smiled. "I'm listening."

"There are things you should know. About the work I do. Why I'm here."

He reached for her hand. "If you're going to tell me you write the Boulderbottom column for *Aspects,* I already know."

She stared at him. "You know about Victoria Boulderbottom?"

"It wasn't hard to figure out." He made a gesture toward the computer. "You work in here every day, and have deadlines every week, yet there's never anything with your byline in the magazine."

He laughed in that self-mocking way she always found so appealing. "Believe me, I've read every issue since I met you, searching for your name." He ran his thumb across her knuckles. "I didn't put it together until last week, when you wrote about the quirks of rich men. What was it you called it?"

She winced, embarrassed. "'King of the Hill and How to Play the Game.'"

"That's it." He bowed his head, looking at their hands. "When I saw myself in the first paragraph, I knew right away that Victoria Boulderbottom was really you."

"I'm sorry—"

"Why? Every word was true. You're very good, Jeannie. That's why I'm sure you'd find the kind of life I can offer you rewarding."

"So you understand what 'Marrying Well' is all about then?"

"Finding a rich husband."

She looked away, unable to face him. "Yes."

He crooked a finger under her chin and brought her back. "Then I believe I qualify."

"Definitely."

He stroked a thumb across her lips. "So what do you say to my proposal?"

She glanced at the darkened monitor. Her heart may have closed around the wrong man, a man who didn't want her, who didn't love her. But her mind was wide open, and it had been telling her for weeks that Stuart Singleton could be the one who'd unlock it again. "Yes," she said, already composing Victoria's victory column in her mind.

Kyle pushed a file across the desk. "Magda Ladanski," he said, pausing while his new publisher flipped back the cover.

"I remember her. Heavy, older lady," Jason said.

"A highly respected professional," Kyle corrected. "She's well-known in the industry and a favorite with readers. You don't want to tick her off, Jason. Ever."

The young man chuckled. "Then I'll have to remember to make nice with Magda Ladanski, won't I? Who's next?"

Satisfied, Kyle moved on, going through the personnel records one by one, making sure Jason understood exactly where he stood. Kyle had spent too long assembling a staff he could trust to risk having Jason make a mistake.

"What's this?" Jason asked when they reached Jeannie's file. "There's nothing here but a résumé and tax forms."

Kyle smiled. "Look again."

Jason went through the pages again. "Nothing. Just this note. 'Watch her.'" He shrugged. "What's that supposed to mean?"

"It mean's she's going to win Pulitzers." Kyle closed the file and laid it on the stack. "Just watch her."

He was picking up the next folder when someone knocked at the door.

Trish poked her head into the office. "Sorry to interrupt, but your flight leaves in two hours, Kyle."

"Thanks, Trish." Kyle turned to Jason. "Why don't you take the rest of these home? I'll call when I get to Bristol Harbor."

"Fine." Jason rose and smoothed his tie. "Have a good trip, Mr. Hunter. And you can count on me to keep everything going just as it is."

Kyle accompanied him to the door. "I never doubted it for a moment, Jason."

Returning to his desk, Kyle locked the drawers and had just started on the filing cabinets when Trish knocked on the door again.

"Someone to see you, Kyle."

He didn't look around. "I'm already late. Tell whoever it is to see Jason."

"This won't take long. I promise."

Her silken voice cut deep, like a razor on a wound that hadn't had time to heal. Kyle turned slowly, telling himself it would be fine. He could do this. But then she smiled, and the aching started all over again. "How are you, Jeannie?"

She shifted her duffel bag from one hand to the other. "I'm fine. How about you?"

The Western clothes looked good on her. A perfect fit. And he wondered briefly if Stuart Singleton had bought them for her.

"Busy," he heard himself say. "You know how it is."

"I heard about Race Week," she said. "I'm sorry you lost."

"It doesn't matter." Nothing mattered. Only that she was here. Kyle walked around behind the desk, hoping to make her feel less awkward. Hoping she'd stay if he kept a distance. "Please sit down."

She stood a moment longer, watching him, then walked to the desk. Finally he could smell her perfume—

something different again. Something he didn't recognize at all.

"Look," she was saying, "I'll keep this brief. Stuart has asked me to marry him. I thought you should know."

Kyle swayed a little, caught himself, then sat down. "And what did you say?"

She hesitated and he couldn't breathe.

"I said yes."

Kyle forced himself to draw in air. "You're in love with him, then."

She nodded, but couldn't hold his gaze, and Kyle knew he'd lost her completely.

Somehow he managed to unlock the desk drawer. To pull out an envelope and set it on the desk. He even smiled. "So you've won. Congratulations."

She glanced down at the envelope. "What's this?"

"The share agreement. Thirty-three percent of the magazine and an expense form. To be paid out of my own pocket if I remember correctly." He rose and held out a hand. "All the best, Jeannie. I hope you'll be happy."

Jeannie saw the callused palm and strong fingers, and the only thing she could think of was the way those hands felt when he held her. She knew if she touched him, she'd forget why she'd left Maine in the first place. And why she was going to marry Stuart.

So she stuffed the envelope into her bag, and Kyle withdrew his hand. "I have something for you, too," she said, and held up a disk. "Victoria Boulderbottom's last column." She set it on the desk between them. "I believe you'll find the tone suitably triumphant."

Kyle picked up the disk, turned it over in his palm. "I'm sure Victoria's fans will love it."

"Yes." Jeannie toyed with the strap on her bag, then turned and headed for the door. "Well, I won't take up any more of your time. I know you've got a flight to catch.''

''Jeannie, wait.''

Her heart began to pound as he came toward her, then sank when he held out only the disk. What else had she expected? A declaration of love? A plea for her to stay? Hardly. He had a flight to catch, after all.

''Just drop this off in Editorial,'' he told her.

Jeannie tried to ignore the rushing in her ears as she tucked the disk into her pocket. ''Don't you want to read it first?''

He turned abruptly. ''I'd rather not.''

Jeannie sat cross-legged on her living room rug, going through her CDs. The smell of pizza drifted in from the kitchen and she could hear Stuart whistling as he rummaged through her cupboards. She got up, plugged in some soft rock then lit a few candles, determined this would be the night.

''Let's see if I've got this straight,'' Stuart said as he folded his legs and sat down across from her. ''The guy with the hair is your brother, Tia gave you the Corvette and that picture on the wall is Lady Victoria Boulderbottom.''

Jeannie wrestled with the strings of cheese on her pizza slice. ''You're a quick study.''

Stuart brushed a bit of sauce from her lip. ''Only where you're concerned.'' He motioned to another picture. ''And who are they?''

Jeannie set her pizza on the plate and studied the shot. ''My parents. They've retired to Florida now, but my mother used to be an opera star.'' She felt herself smile. ''Would you like to hear her album?''

''Maybe later,'' Stuart said with a sheepish grin. ''I'm afraid I'm not much of an opera fan.''

Jeannie reached for the pizza. "That's okay. We've got a lifetime to listen to it."

Stuart took her plate and slid it to one side. "I like the way you're thinking."

Jeannie cleared her throat and drew her plate back. "Well, that's what marriage is all about, isn't it?"

He set the plate well out of reach this time. "That's exactly what it's about. Being together."

She watched him lift her hand, kiss her fingertips, her palm, her wrist. It was pleasant, warm, comforting even. But something was missing. She cast a quick, desperate glance around the room.

More candles. That had to be it. She inched back along the rug. "Would you excuse me a minute?"

Stuart let her hands drop. "What now?"

"Candles." She scrambled to her feet and dashed to the kitchen.

"But there are plenty in here now."

"There's always room for more." Yanking open the bottom drawer, Jeannie pulled out a box of sturdy white candles, the ones she kept in case of emergencies. She tore at the plastic wrapping with her teeth. If there was ever an emergency, this was it.

Stuart stood in the doorway, watching her. "Jeannie," he said softly. "What's going on?"

She spit out the plastic bits and shoved her hair out of her face. "Nothing. Everything's fine. You'll see."

He came toward her. "All I see right now is a woman who's trying hard to convince herself of something. Jeannie, tell me what's wrong."

Her shoulders sagged as she walked past him into the living room. There was no use trying to fool herself any longer. She couldn't marry Stuart and she knew it. Not when she didn't love him.

Kyle had been right all along, she realized. The whole

idea of marrying well was ridiculous. She glanced up at the picture on the wall. And Victoria would just have to understand.

She laid the box of candles on the coffee table. "Sit down, Stuart. We have to talk."

Even through the heavy apartment door, Magda's tone was unmistakable. Someone was in real trouble.

"...if you forgot the fortune cookies again, you can turn right around right and—" She swung the door open and froze midthreat. "Kyle? What are you doing here?"

He held out his empty hands. "Not getting a tip, I'd say."

"That's for sure." Recovered, she leaned a shoulder against the frame and crossed her arms. "Aren't you supposed to be in Maine?"

"I was." He let his hands drop, realizing this wasn't going to be as easy as he'd hoped. "I need to know where Jeannie is."

"Why?"

"It's a long story. Is she in Alaska or Montana?"

"Neither." She tilted her head to the side. "You haven't read her latest column, have you?" Kyle shook his head and Magda nodded knowingly. "Last I heard, she was staying in a little place with a god-awful kitchen, but a great garage."

"Are you saying she's in Chicago?"

"Clever boy."

"Who's with her?"

Magda shrugged. "I forget."

"But you do remember the pet shows."

"All right, she's alone."

"Are you sure?"

"Am I ever wrong?" Magda pointed a finger. "And if you hurt her again, Kyle Hunter—"

"Magda, I love her."

The finger curled back as a smile spread across her face. "So, he finally admits it. I knew all along, of course. As a matter of fact—"

"Magda."

"Hmm?"

"I hear summer in England is wonderful. Why don't you take a week or two and cover the theater season?"

She closed one eye. "First-class?"

"First-class."

She let out a whoop. "Kippers for breakfast. I can taste them now."

"One other thing," Kyle said as he was leaving. "Don't say anything to Jeannie."

Magda smiled. "You know me, Kyle."

13

He pulled up in front of the house. There were no lights on, only the glow of candles through the windows. Kyle felt his stomach slide. Maybe Magda had been wrong. Maybe Stuart was still there.

He took the stairs two at a time and listened at the door. No voices, but he could hear music—soft rock, the aphrodisiac of choice.

Kyle knocked. When there was no answer, he tried the handle. It wasn't locked. She was either careless or expecting someone. He swallowed hard and pushed open the door.

A line of tiny votive candles ran from the front door along the hall and into the kitchen. Kyle's heart began to pound. She was definitely expecting someone. Someone close. Someone who might already be there, and had just forgotten to lock the door behind him.

What kind of fool would forget the lock when he was greeted by something like this? Kyle nudged the door closed and followed the footpath of candlelight.

And found her in the darkened kitchen.

She stood by the table, her hair loose, her feet and shoulders bare beneath a dress of sheerest summer cotton, the row of tiny buttons fastened from bodice to hem.

"Aren't you supposed to be in Maine?" she asked, her

voice low and husky in the dark, just as he remembered it.

She rested her hands on the table and leaned back, drawing his gaze down to the swell of her breasts, the soft plane of her belly, the full curve of her hips. Kyle couldn't move. So he propped a hand against the door frame and hoped for the best.

"Aren't you supposed to be with Stuart?" he answered.

She lifted one shoulder. Let it fall. "Change in plans."

"Same here." He tried to moisten his lips but found his mouth too dry. He glanced at the candles on the counter, and wondered what perfume she wore. "Looks like you're expecting company."

"I could be." She undid the top button of her dress and smiled. Kyle thought his heart would stop.

"Why don't you tell me why you're here?" she asked.

The only answer that came to mind right then was to kiss her. To feel that impudent mouth soften and open in the way he knew so well. But he took a deep breath instead, and tried to remember the speech he'd been rehearsing since he left Maine.

"Jeannie, I'm sorry. I was wrong, about everything."

She tilted her head and flipped open another button. "Go on."

Kyle shuffled his feet, adjusted his stance—not sure he liked the challenge in her eyes. "After you left, I figured I could get over you. That being in Bristol Harbor would make the wanting go away. But it didn't work."

She slid another button through another loop, and Kyle saw that she wore nothing underneath.

Her fingertips circled the next button. "Tell me why."

"Why?" He rubbed a hand over his mouth, trying hard to keep his thoughts straight. "Because nothing was right without you. Not the boat, the trip, none of it. And because the water kept laughing at me, for being such a fool."

He took a single step toward her, but she held up a hand, stopping him. "Go on," she said, pressing the dress close to her breasts as she slipped one slender strap over her shoulder.

"No one makes me feel the way you do, Jeannie," he groaned.

She undid another button and let the dress slide a little lower. "I'm listening."

"I can't go back to Maine without you. I can't be on the boat, I can't sleep in my bed." He pushed a hand through his hair. "Jeannie, I'm dying here."

"Good." She turned her back, her eyes holding him as she let the dress fall to her waist. Her skin was smooth and golden in the candlelight, and Kyle's fingers clenched as she slowly ran a hand up and down her arm. "You were saying?"

He cleared his throat. "I was saying that if you won't come to Maine with me, I'll stay here, because I need you. And I love you. I've loved you from the day you slapped that first fifty dollars down and dared me to pick it up." He paused, barely breathing. "I only hope I'm not too late."

Jeannie watched him a moment longer, her heart beating fast, every part of her aching to go to him. But she wanted more from him this time. Much more. She let the dress fall to the floor, shivering at the first brush of night through the open window, then she turned to him.

Her breath caught as his gaze raked over her, the love

he felt so clear in his eyes, his face, his tortured, clenching fingers, making her feel beautiful, sensual, strong.

She moved toward him, slowly, softly. "Tell me what you want, Kyle."

He lifted his gaze. "All I want is you. And a houseful of kids and a shelf full of Pulitzers. What I mean is…" He stopped, moistened his lips and tried again. "What I mean is, Jeannie, will you marry me?"

Jeannie watched him, feeling her heart open all over again, taking him deep inside this time and locking the door firmly behind him.

"Of course I will," she whispered. "But only because I love you."

And suddenly he was all over her, powerful arms pulling her close while hard hands rocked her hips against him. Jeannie heard him mutter something about perfume and Magda and pet shows as he buried his face in her neck. Then she closed her eyes and abandoned herself to sensation, feeling herself melting into him, becoming part of him, part of everything he was.

"So when do we leave?" she murmured, frowning a little when his mouth left her breast.

"Leave?"

"For the Seychelles, the Antilles. And where was that other place?" She opened her eyes to find him looking down at her, puzzled. "You don't think you're going without me, do you?" she demanded.

A smile eased across his face. "Not a chance. Not now. Not ever."

She snapped her fingers as warm hands lifted her up onto the table. "That's it."

"That's what?"

"The name for the boat. *Not Now. Not Ever.*"

"We'll talk about it later," Kyle whispered, then covered her mouth with his, quickly clearing any notions of boats and names from her mind.

"I guess you know what this means, then, don't you?" she murmured as he gently laid her back.

"It means you win."

"Uh-huh." She sighed and wrapped her arms around him, pulling him down. "And you get to drive."

* * * * *

Take 4 bestselling love stories FREE

Plus get a FREE surprise gift!

Special Limited-time Offer

Mail to Silhouette Reader Service™

3010 Walden Avenue
P.O. Box 1867
Buffalo, N.Y. 14269-1867

YES! Please send me 4 free Silhouette Yours Truly™ novels and my free surprise gift. Then send me 4 brand-new novels every other month, which I will receive months before they appear in bookstores. Bill me at the low price of $2.69 each plus 25¢ delivery and applicable sales tax, if any.* That's the complete price and a savings of over 10% off the cover prices—quite a bargain! I understand that accepting the books and gift places me under no obligation ever to buy any books. I can always return a shipment and cancel at any time. Even if I never buy another book from Silhouette, the 4 free books and the surprise gift are mine to keep forever.

201 BPA AZH2

Name	(PLEASE PRINT)	
Address	Apt. No.	
City	State	Zip

This offer is limited to one order per household and not valid to present Silhouette Yours Truly™ subscribers. *Terms and prices are subject to change without notice. Sales tax applicable in N.Y.

USYRT-296

©1996 Harlequin Enterprises Limited

As seen on TV!
Free Gift Offer

With a Free Gift proof-of-purchase from any Silhouette® book,
you can receive a beautiful cubic zirconia pendant.

This gorgeous marquise-shaped stone is a genuine cubic
zirconia—accented by an 18" gold tone necklace.

(Approximate retail value $19.95)

Send for yours today...
compliments of ▼ *Silhouette*®
TM

To receive your free gift, a cubic zirconia pendant, send us one original proof-of-purchase, photocopies not accepted, from the back of any Silhouette Romance™, Silhouette Desire®, Silhouette Special Edition®, Silhouette Intimate Moments® or Silhouette Yours Truly™ title available in February, March and April at your favorite retail outlet, together with the Free Gift Certificate, plus a check or money order for $1.65 U.S./$2.15 CAN. (do not send cash) to cover postage and handling, payable to Silhouette Free Gift Offer. We will send you the specified gift. Allow 6 to 8 weeks for delivery. Offer good until April 30, 1997 or while quantities last. Offer valid in the U.S. and Canada only.

Free Gift Certificate

Name: _____

Address: _____

City: _____ State/Province: _____ Zip/Postal Code: _____

Mail this certificate, one proof-of-purchase and a check or money order for postage and handling to: SILHOUETTE FREE GIFT OFFER 1997. In the U.S.: 3010 Walden Avenue, P.O. Box 9077, Buffalo NY 14269-9077. In Canada: P.O. Box 613, Fort Erie, Ontario L2Z 5X3.

FREE GIFT OFFER   084-KFD
ONE PROOF-OF-PURCHASE
To collect your fabulous FREE GIFT, a cubic zirconia pendant, you must include this
original proof-of-purchase for each gift with the properly completed Free Gift Certificate.

084-KFD